D0354381

Other books by

JEAN FERRIS

Amen, Moses Gardenia

The Stainless Steel Rule

Invincible Summer

Looking for Home

Across the Grain

Relative Strangers

Signs of Life

ALL THAT GLITTERS

JEAN FERRIS

ALL THAT GLITTERS

Farrar Straus Giroux • New York

Library of Congress Cataloging-in-Publication Data

Ferris, Jean, date.
    All that glitters / Jean Ferris. — 1st ed.
        p.   cm.
    Summary: When he visits his father in the Florida Keys,
sixteen-year-old Brian is befriended by a local captain who
involves him in the search for a centuries-old sunken ship
and gives him insight into several difficult personal relation-
ships.
    ISBN 0-374-30204-9
    [1. Buried treasure—Fiction. 2. Fathers—Fiction.
3. Interpersonal relations—Fiction. 4. Florida Keys (Fla.)—
Fiction.] I. Title.
PZ7.F4174A1   1996
[Fic]—dc20   95-590

ALL THAT GLITTERS

ONE

Leo, my father, is at the Miami airport in wrinkled white shorts and a wrinkled flowered shirt. He's deeply tanned, as always, but his playboy good looks seem more blurred than I remember from last year, and the skin under his eyes is puffy.

Of course, I'm feeling pretty blurred and puffy myself from all the champagne I drank yesterday at my mother's wedding reception, and from getting up too early this morning to make my plane for my annual visit to Leo; a visit that will last six long weeks this time instead of my usual interminable two, to accommodate Mom's European honeymoon. Sure, I kicked about it, but she wouldn't let me stay with Josh, even though I told her that with six kids in his house already, his parents wouldn't even notice one more.

"Hey, Brian," Leo says, clapping his hand on my

shoulder. He's always done that, even when I was a kid. Now that I'm almost seventeen, I don't think much about it, but I used to wonder why he didn't hug me.

"Flight okay?" he asks. "You look a little under the weather."

"I'm okay," I say, even though my head aches so much I can hardly open my eyes.

"So Laura really got married yesterday?" he says. "Or did somebody in the audience jump up and yell, 'Stop everything! She's impossible!' I've always wanted to see that happen."

"Nobody jumped up," I say. Actually, I guess it was a nice wedding. There were a lot of flowers and champagne, and Mom acted giddy and happy. The Guy, which is what my new stepfather thinks I should call him, didn't say much, just looked photogenic and shook hands a lot and kept calling me pal. "And she's not that impossible." It's true Mom has a pushy aspect to her personality but, hey, she's had to take care of herself and me for a long time: since I was three and she and Leo split up. That attitude has come in handy.

"Well, now you've got a new father," Leo says as we board the escalator to the baggage claim area.

"Stepfather," I say, though that's not a word the Guy, whose name is really Bill, prefers, which is why I'm supposed to call him the Guy.

"You like him?"

"He's all right." He is, I guess. Mom thinks so, and she's a pretty good judge of character. This stepfather stuff gets to me, though. Whether he likes it or not, whatever he calls himself, he *is* my stepfather. He may say I'm getting too old to be anybody's child, but there are still times I'd like to have a father around. And it's sure not going to be Leo.

"I understand he's loaded," Leo says.

"I guess so," I say. "But that's not why she married him. Her business is doing fine." She has a computer company that specializes in rescuing data for people who have messed up their hard drives big time. She has more work than she can handle.

"Well, she made sure she didn't get another one like me. That's a mistake she made only once."

I can't respond to that, so I shift my carry-on camera bag to my other hand and snatch my suitcase off the carousel, and we head for the parking lot.

The air outside the automatic doors falls on me like a weight, moist and thick and superheated.

"Jesus," Leo says. "You never get used to this weather."

He's right. I always forget what June in Florida is like. I wonder how I'm going to survive six weeks here when two is already too long. I guess I'll be watching a lot of TV reruns, the way I always do. At least this year, Leo is living in the same house he did last year. That's a first. He's always lived in Florida, but restlessly, moving around from town to town, sometimes in the Keys, sometimes on the mainland, each place looking like somewhere you'd go on the lam in a forties movie.

Beads of perspiration spring from every sweat gland I have, and I feel as if I'm pushing my way through soup. By the time we reach the pickup, my hair is damp and stuck to my head, which is about to explode, and my shirt is soaked.

I swing my suitcase into the bed of the truck while

Leo unlocks the doors. I carry my camera bag into the cab with me. I've brought my cameras just because I take them everywhere, but I've already photographed Florida hundreds of times and it's a subject that doesn't interest me anymore. The air conditioner roars into action when the ignition is turned, but seems powerless against the weight and heat of what passes for air down here.

"You eat on the plane?" Leo asks, raising his voice over the air-conditioning.

"Yeah." I'd eaten the roll and the gluey dessert. I couldn't face the meat, whatever it was.

My stomach growls loudly.

Leo makes a sound I think is a laugh. "Growing boy, aren't you? We'll pull through the next burger place. I don't want to stop, not when the AC is just getting going. You want fries?"

I occupy myself with burgers, fries, and a chocolate shake while Leo drives in silence, a toothpick in the corner of his mouth and country music blaring from the radio, drowning out the possibility of conversation even if either of us should try to make some, which we don't. My headache subsides after the administration of medicinal fast food.

Eventually Route 1 brings us through the savannahs and mangrove swamps of the Everglades, across Jewfish Creek and Lake Surprise to the sign with the leaping sailfish that announces we're entering the Keys. Immediately after that sign is another one stating HELL IS TRUTH SEEN TOO LATE, whatever that means.

Driving down the Keys is once again a shock. I live

in Chicago, a city next to an enormous lake; I'm used to seeing water. But not water like this, water that's the dominant element, that makes the land seem insignificant. Which it is. The highest point of land in the Keys is only eighteen feet above the water, which isn't much even when you're standing on top of it.

The green-and-white mile markers wind down from No. 109 at Lake Surprise across bridges and through towns full of funky eating places and motels, marinas and dive shops, to No. 47 where the Seven Mile Bridge begins.

I can't help it—driving over that bridge always makes me nervous. Seven miles of water with only a thin bridge with a hump in the middle between me and it. It takes me a while to realize I'm holding my breath. When I exhale, Leo looks at me and then away. The glare off so much water brings back the throb in my head.

Before reaching Bahia Honda, we turn off Route 1 onto the causeway to Mosquito Key, stuck like an orphan out in the Straits of Florida.

The road is bordered with thick, tangled vegetation, sea grape and palmetto, morning glories and joewood, which thins some as we come into Fortunata. The sand flies around here are so ferocious they're known locally as "flying teeth." A cloud of them splatters itself on Leo's windshield.

"Local welcome custom," he says without removing his toothpick. "Effective but messy." This is the first thing he's said in almost three hours.

Fortunata isn't much: one main street of three or four blocks, a scatter of cottages and trailer homes on crushed-limestone lanes, and, behind the main street, the water. At the water's edge are docks for pleasure boats and the boats that take tourists fishing when the opportunity presents itself and fish commercially the rest of the time. One of them is the *Crazy Conch*, Leo's boat.

We turn right, onto the main street, passing a bar, a mini-grocery, a Laundromat, and I remember these places. Then we turn left, onto one of the limestone lanes, and come to a stop at Leo's weathered frame cottage facing the water. It looks tireder than last year. It's old enough so that it's not up on stilts, the way the newer houses have to be, to let the storm winds and waters pass through. Somehow it seems just like Leo to pick a house that ignores any commonsense regard for what the future might bring.

Leo jumps out of the truck. "It may not look like much, but the rent's paid, so it's home." It's the same thing he said last summer.

When I open the truck door, the rush of humid, fish-scented air feels like a slap with a wet mackerel. I pull my suitcase out over the side of the truck bed and follow Leo into the house through the kitchen door.

The blinds are pulled and the window air conditioner roars and rattles. It's barely cooler inside than out.

"Excuse the mess," Leo says. "I meant to clean up, but . . ." He makes an offhand gesture. "Something always seems to interfere." He looks at me. "I know what your mother'd say."

So do I.

The place looks just the way it did the day I left last year: sink full of dishes, table tattooed with the rings of glasses and coffee cups, drifts of newspapers beside the brown corduroy recliner in front of the TV, fishing poles propped in the corner. A ripe aroma indicates the trash needs to be taken out.

"It looks like I remember it," I say.

Leo gives a short laugh. "Yeah, I guess it does. Well, that's what I call decor around here."

I can't explain why Leo's mess means lack of discipline, a slovenly mentality, and unsanitary habits, while my equally messy room at home, with my computer stuff and camera equipment, clothes and sports gear all over the place, means comfort, creativity, and a piquant sort of carelessness. Here, of course, my room will be militarily neat. In no way am I like my father. And I want him to know it.

"I'm in the same place as last year?" I ask, lugging my bags down the hall. The room smells faintly of mildew. The mattress is bare, though there is a pillow and clean folded sheets at its foot. The bureau, too, is bare, and the wooden chair between it and the bed is the only other piece of furniture. A can of air freshener stands on the chair.

The chair and the bureau are dust-free and the linoleum floor is spotless. I wonder who cleaned it up. Leo is not my first guess.

Leo stands in the doorway. "Use the spray. It smells a little funny in here."

"Okay."

"After you unpack, we can go to town, have some supper, and watch the sunset."

Go to town means walking about two blocks.

"Okay," I say again. I've learned that watching sunsets is a very big deal in the Keys, a daily drama that people stop whatever they're doing to look at. I open my suitcase and take out piles of T-shirts, underwear, shorts, a lot of them new. Mom has equipped me for this trip as if I'm going on a honeymoon, too. I wonder how much of it is for me and how much is for Leo: a kind of in-your-face announcement of how well she, and now, by implication, the Guy, look after me.

I put the clothes into the bureau drawers. I shut the drawers and then open them again, checking to be sure the piles are squared and tidy. I make the bed and squirt a cloud of Summer Surprise around before I leave.

TWO

Captain Hook's is the only real restaurant in Fortunata, so that's where we go, just as we did the first night last summer. It's pretty hard to get excited about eating in a place that has a sign over the door saying WE APOLOGIZE IN ADVANCE.

A waitress wearing a name tag that reads PeeWee seats us at a table for four on the screened porch facing the water, after giving Leo a complicated look that seems to combine fury and longing. When she's silently thrown menus down on the table and stalked away, Leo shrugs and says, "She must be upset about something."

I'm pretty sure Leo knows why she's upset, but I don't want to hear about it.

"Have what you want." Leo waves the menu magnanimously. "Shrimp, lobster, whatever. Anything."

I don't really like seafood—another thing that makes

me feel like such a misfit down here where seafood is either on your plate or at the end of your fishing line or before the faceplate of your snorkeling mask.

"I'll have the fish and chips," I say. The only way I can get fish down is when it's fried in a lot of batter.

"Oh, come on," Leo says. "Have the bugs."

Bugs are crayfish, things that, even cooked, don't look edible, but that Leo, for some reason, considers a great delicacy.

"I'll have the fish and chips," I say again.

Leo makes one of those sounds in his throat that I can never interpret and returns to his menu, which he must know by heart.

"Hey, Leo," a voice calls from a party PeeWee is leading onto the porch.

Leo looks up. "Hey, Nathan. Hi, Lisbon, Tia. You having dinner?"

Nathan, a tall man with skin the color of ebony, a tiny gold ring in one ear, and a face that looks as if it has been carved from stone with primitive tools, laughs. "No, man. We come in here looking for a tennis game. What do you think we're doing here?" His voice is as rich and resonant as a church organ, and I remember seeing him last summer on an immaculate white boat whose name, *Angelfish*, suddenly jumps into my mind. He's hard to miss or to forget.

"Well, join us. This is my son, Brian. He's visiting again."

The way he says "again" sounds to me as if I pop down all the time, making a nuisance of myself.

"Hello, Brian," Nathan says, sticking out his hand. When I take it, my hand almost disappears in his.

1 2

"This here is Lisbon Doucette," he says, indicating a caramel-colored woman with the face of a Christmas card angel, "and her daughter, Tia." Lisbon shakes my hand with her cool, slim one, and Tia raises her hand in a half-salute.

I've already noticed Tia's mass of curly hair, piled up somehow on her head, and her skin, the color of coffee with cream, but until she gets closer I don't register her copper-gold eyes and the multiple silver hoops in each of her ears.

"Hi," I say. She's probably the most beautiful girl of my own age I've ever seen, and that fact dries up my powers of speech.

"Hi," she says and drops into the extra chair she's pulled over from another table. Even though she doesn't seem to be trying, her body behaves with the grace of a cat's.

She stretches her smooth bare legs under the table and leans back, looking preoccupied, as if she's solving calculus problems in her head.

"Leo been looking forward to you coming," Nathan says.

"He has?" I say. I figured Mom had to bribe him with something good to get him to keep me longer than the two weeks he was already stuck with.

"Sure," Nathan says. "You ought to tell your boy that yourself sometime," he adds to Leo.

Leo makes a sound with an inflection that is neither positive nor negative and, as usual, I don't know what he means.

After we order from a sullen PeeWee, who seems annoyed at having to reset our table, Lisbon says to me,

"You know, this isn't the best time to be in the Keys. Not as a tourist, anyway. We natives like it 'cause it makes us feel so superior. We don't mind the humidity and the insects and the hurricanes. We got starch in us; not just in our backbones, but in our whole skeletons." She laughs, the church-bell accompaniment to Nathan's pipe-organ guffaw.

"Miss Tia," Nathan says, "you could put some of that starch in your backbone. Looks like you're about to go under the table."

She straightens up fractionally, the kind of movement you make so that you can continue to do what was annoying someone else and still say, "But I *did* what you said," in an aggrieved tone of voice. I know those tricks.

"Maybe you'll be lucky for us," Lisbon says to me, "and we'll find the *Nueva Cádiz* while you're here."

"What's the *Nueva Cádiz*?" I ask.

"Why, Leo." Lisbon looks at my father, her eyes surprised.

"I'd have gotten to it," Leo says.

What was wrong with those silent hours from the airport in Miami to Fortunata if he had something he wanted to tell me? I wait. So do Lisbon and Nathan. It's impossible to know if Tia does or not.

Leo turns to me. "There's a guy down here this summer, a Dr. Rafe Ryker, he's an archaeologist from the U. of Florida, who's looking for a Spanish galleon off Fortunata, one that sank in 1648. That kind of stuff, treasure hunting, goes on all the time down here."

Nathan shakes his head, exasperated. "The real news is, my boat, the *Angelfish*, and your daddy's *Crazy Conch* have been hired for the whole summer for the search. We'll make as much as we could have made from commercial fishing and tourist trips, maybe more, and we'll be in on the hunt. You know anybody who hasn't wanted to find sunken treasure?"

I've never thought about it before, but suddenly *I* want to find it, too. Sunken treasure: the lure and promise of riches waiting for the right person. The deserving person. Me.

"That's great," I say. "How do you look for sunken treasure? I don't know anything about it."

"Well, Rafe would be the one to ask. He's staying at Lisbon's place—she runs the End of the Rainbow, the finest guesthouse on Mosquito Key—"

Lisbon laughs and slaps his arm. "You know it's the only guesthouse on Mosquito Key."

He puts his big hand over hers. "In all the Keys, then. Anyway, he's staying there getting things ready. We'll be starting in a couple days. Your daddy and I are both going to dive for him. Miss Tia, too, if she wants to. She's been playing a tad hard to get."

She gives him a scowl that should hurt, and he growls at her and then laughs. She doesn't say anything.

"You're diving?" I look at Nathan and Leo and Tia in that order.

"Hey," Nathan says. "Don't be so surprised. We ain't the Three Stooges, you know. It's pretty common, so I hear, for treasure hunters to use local diving clubs and such to help. They're cheaper than pros, and most of these search outfits are always short of money. Rafe, he's on a real shoestring. Had a hard time getting any funding at all because most people who might know, he tells me, think the *Nueva Cádiz* is nowhere near Fortunata."

"I took some scuba lessons last spring," I say tentatively. I only took them to please Mom, who gave them to me for my birthday. I knew at the time she was looking for a way to make my Florida stays more fun, but I haven't been grateful until now.

"Well, talk to Rafe," Nathan says. "I can't see where another pair of hands would hurt, but he's the boss and it's his checkbook."

"You any good at it?" Tia asks, still slumped, her hands clasped on her stomach. She looks at me sideways.

"Good enough," I say, stung by the disdain in her voice, all the more because I know I'm not anywhere near experienced enough to be much help in a search like this. Two dives in frigid, murky Lake Michigan probably aren't preparation for anything except a little bragging.

"Tia's an excellent diver," Lisbon says. "Most fish don't swim as well as she does."

"Don't," Tia says to her mother.

"Well," Lisbon says, "anybody's who's grown up on Florida beaches *better* be a good swimmer or something's wrong."

There's a tension between Tia and Lisbon and Nathan that thickens as I watch. It's clear that Lisbon and Nathan are involved with each other, but I don't think Nathan is Tia's father—he'd introduced her as Lisbon's daughter. But he has a father's proprietary manner about her—or what I assume is a father's proprietary manner. How would I know?

PeeWee arrives with a tray as big as a picnic table, supported by thin arms that seem to be all muscle. She plunks the plates down in front of us like an impatient card dealer, grabs her tray, and goes away fast, her rubber soles squeaking on the linoleum floor.

Tia reaches out and takes a french fry from my plate without changing her slouch in the chair. She eats it leisurely, in about twelve tiny bites, and then takes another one.

"What's the story on the *Nueva Cádiz*?" I ask, pretending to ignore her looting. I ask Nathan, not Leo, who holds on to his information as if *it's* sunken treasure. "What kind of treasure does it have?"

"The usual, from what I understand. Silver, gold, jewels. But Rafe, he's an archaeologist, not a banker. That's not the most interesting part to him, even if it would be to almost anybody else, me included." He smiles, his white teeth so strong-looking it seems he should have ordered a chunk of raw meat for dinner instead of shrimp.

"Why does he think it's near here if no one else does?"

"You better ask him that," Nathan says. "How about you let me check you out on scuba tomorrow—just so I can give him a good recommendation for you—and then maybe we can sweet-talk Lisbon into making us some breakfast and you can meet the Doc."

"Sure," I say. I don't even look in Leo's direction. If he wants me to do something with him tomorrow, he'll have to say so.

He doesn't.

"I was a SEAL in the Navy," Nathan says, "so I can put you through some hoops underwater. You up for it?"

"You trying to scare me?"

17

Nathan laughs his big laugh. "A waste of time, I can see that. We're going to enjoy tomorrow."

It's odd, but I already feel as if I know Nathan better than I know Leo.

The ball of the sun is just touching the horizon, and it seems close enough to walk to.

"Oh," Lisbon says, "just look at that! Don't you expect to see clouds of steam when that hot sun touches the water? Have you ever seen the green flash, Brian?"

"What's that?"

"Leo, you've neglected your son's education." She sounds disapproving. "Well, you watch," she says to me. "When the sun goes just beneath the horizon, sometimes the light rays bend or something and there's a flash of neon-green light. It's pretty rare, but I've seen it twice. You'll have to watch every sunset while you're here, and I bet you'll see one."

We're all silent as the sun disappears, but there's no green flash. I wonder if that's why sunset is such a big deal in the Keys. Or if this green flash is something perpetrated by natives on visitors, like snipe-hunting or shell games.

"What time you want to get up, Brian?" Nathan asks me when the sun is gone. "You a late or an early person?"

I often stay up way too late at home, playing video games and dinking around with my computer, or trying new techniques in the darkroom, but I still usually wake up early. Maybe I'm a morning person, even though that description sounds perkier than I think I am.

"I like the morning," I say.

"Fine, fine, it's the best time, the freshest."

"What time?"

"How's seven? First we work, then we go to Lisbon's and beg her to fix us one of her breakfasts. I tell you, her cooking can make dead men walk."

"You're welcome for breakfast anytime, Brian," Lisbon say. "Once in a while you can even bring your big friend, Nathan."

THREE

The roar of the air conditioner translates into the sound of waves on a beach in my dreams. All night I dream of struggling in deep water, of trying to breathe air that isn't there, of meeting sharks and barracuda with mayhem on their minds.

I wake at six, tired from my water dreams. In my undershorts, camera in hand, I pad through the house and out the kitchen door. The beach is only steps away, and I walk down to it in air that's warm but not yet oppressive.

I never get over expecting wide, white California-travel-poster-style beaches, always forgetting that real beaches in the Keys are rare: what they are is small, narrow patches at the water's edge, hemmed in by vegetation and made of ground-up coral. That's the way the one outside Leo's cottage is. I take a picture, but I don't spend enough time setting it up and I know it won't turn out well.

I go down to stand in the water, which must be close to 98.6 degrees, since I can hardly tell where my skin leaves off and the water begins. My feet look long and white and delicate under the water and the rough coral sand hurts them. I take a shot of them. I find myself not wanting Tia to see me in a bathing suit. My physique is okay, but it's so city-white. And she's so gold and tawny, so healthy and glowing. I frown down at my feet. She's also, from the vibes I picked up last night at Captain Hook's, trouble.

I look up into the sky, still with the haze of night on it, and then out to the horizon, where sea and sky meet and blur. I try to imagine a ship under that water, one that has lain there for three hundred and fifty years, full of skeletons and treasure. Thinking about it makes me hungry, so I go in.

The cornflakes are damp from the humidity and the milk has a suspicious smell, but a banana and some sugar help. I wash my dishes, dry them, and set them neatly in the cupboard before I put on my trunks, a layer of sunscreen, a T-shirt, and rubber flip-flops and head off to meet Nathan.

"Hello, Brian," Nathan booms as I come out onto the dock where the *Angelfish* is secured. He wears only a small nylon swimsuit from which a magnificent muscled torso rises. I wonder if I really have to take off my T-shirt.

"Hi," I say.

"You ready to get wet?" Nathan asks.

"Sure." I hesitate and then rush on. "I should probably tell you, I just took lessons this spring. In Chicago. I've really only dived twice, if you don't count the practice in the pool." I stop, wondering if I have to tell him the rest: that I didn't want to seem incompetent in front of Tia.

"And?" Nathan prompts.

"And it was . . . I don't know . . . weird. Dark and not much going on." I wait for Nathan to say something about the false impression I deliberately gave him.

"Well, it's a lot different here," Nathan says, arranging two sets of snorkels and masks, scuba tanks, and other gear. "And then some. You got some big surprises coming to you." After a pause he says, "I don't know of a man alive who hasn't said something he regrets, trying to impress a woman. Now let's see what you can do."

We spend a while fitting flippers and weight belts and buoyancy compensators. I've forgotten how strange it is to breathe through a regulator, and how stretched my mouth would feel for the rest of the day after a lesson.

Nathan asks me a lot of questions about emergency ascents and how to recognize anoxia and read underwater hand signals, and then we go in. I'm surprised I remember so much of that stuff.

We snorkel around the dock, looking down at sand and pilings and nothing else, getting used to the water before we go under.

From my first lesson, I've had a terror, those first few panicky underwater breaths, that the regulator won't work. It isn't a natural thing, this breathing underwater, and until I see that flurry of bubbles rising past my face, I'm tense and scared. Then I remember it really is possible to breathe underwater, as long as I don't try to inhale through my nose.

Nathan watches me get my breathing rhythm started, then gives me a thumbs-up and signals me to follow him. We pass the bulk of the *Angelfish* and the last piers of the dock and move out into deeper water, the sound of my own breathing loud in my ears.

Shafts of sunlight penetrate the pale water, reflecting in wavering paths of gold along the sandy bottom. Because there is no reef or wreck here, the places fish like to congregate, there isn't much to look at, but it's already the best scuba experience I've ever had. For one thing, the water is warm, unlike Lake Michigan, which never is, and for another, I can see, which I couldn't in Lake Michigan. The water is so clear I could have read a newspaper on the bottom, fifteen feet down.

I kick along, turning when Nathan does, drifting into a kind of trance, lulled by the mantra of my own breathing and by the dreamlike gold and silver and blue world around me, forgetting to think about anything.

Suddenly I'm in front of the dock again, the shadow of *Angelfish* over my shoulder. The spell of the warm, sunlit water is broken, and when Nathan motions to ascend, I follow.

I pull myself up the ladder to the dock.

"Ah, I recognize that look," Nathan says, helping me off with my tank. "You're in love, boy."

"I guess I am. That was really something. Not at all like diving in Lake Michigan."

Nathan snorts. "That was really nothing. Wait'll I take you where there's something to see. Fish that eat out of your hands and wrecks where people young as you met their ends. Coral in shapes you can't believe and herds of rays flapping up the bottom sand. It's another planet out there."

"When?" I ask.

Nathan laughs. "Soon as we can."

FOUR

Lisbon's guesthouse is a gingerbready, cupolaed Queen Anne with conch architecture additions, Nathan explains to me: jalousied doors, top-hung shutters, and wrap-around porches on both levels, painted lavender with purple and indigo trim.

In the big, airy kitchen, Tia sits at the square oak kitchen table in a one-piece bathing suit drinking coffee from a huge cup and reading. Lisbon sits across from her making a shopping list. When we come in, Lisbon looks up, but Tia doesn't.

I can smell cinnamon and apples and I suddenly start salivating so much I'm afraid I'm going to drool down the front of my T-shirt.

Lisbon shakes her head. "How many times do I have to tell you not to slam that back door, Nathan?"

He drops a kiss on the top of her head. "Sorry. One look at you and my head is filled only with love."

Lisbon laughs her luxurious laugh and stands. "You are awful. I suppose you're wanting some breakfast now."

"We wouldn't turn some down, would we, Brian? Anyway, we have cause for celebration. Our friend Brian is a scuba natural. He'll be a fine help to the Doc."

"Wonderful," Tia says without looking up. "So he won't be needing me."

"Miss Tia," Nathan says in an ominous tone of voice. "You know he needs all the help he can get." He softens his voice with an effort. "And you are an excellent diver."

She looks up, straight at him. "Well, I ought to be. You taught me. And you won't take anything less." She goes back to her book, but I doubt she's really reading.

I can't figure out if what she's said to Nathan is a compliment or an insult.

Nathan and Lisbon exchange an expressive look while I stand awkwardly by. Then Lisbon puts her hand on my shoulder. "This boy's hungry," she says. "I'd better feed him."

She goes to work at the stove. "You just missed Rafe, Brian," Lisbon says. "He went off to Key West for something, but he'll be back tonight. How'd you like to come have some supper with us?"

"Sure, great," I say, though the prospect of sitting at the same table for breakfast and dinner with somebody acting like Tia, no matter how good she looks, doesn't exactly thrill me. I wonder if Lisbon is going to include my father in the dinner invitation, but she doesn't say anything about him and I'm not going to ask.

Lisbon takes a tray of mammoth apple-cinnamon rolls

out of the oven, piles a few of them on a plate, and puts it in the middle of the table along with pots of jam and butter, a bowl of fresh fruit, and a plate of fried ham with scrambled eggs.

"Sit," she says. "You want coffee or tea, hot or cold? Or milk? Or juice?"

"Milk's fine," I say, overwhelmed by all these choices. At home, it's cereal and O.J. every day.

"Iced coffee," Nathan says. "You know how I like it."

"I know all right," Lisbon says. "Enough cream to make your arteries holler, and sugar on top of that."

Nathan smacks his lips. "Stop talking about it and get me some, woman," he says.

"With that attitude, you can get it yourself." Lisbon pours herself a glass of iced tea, brings my milk, and sits down at the table.

Nathan, laughing, finds the iced coffee, cream, and sugar and fixes his own drink. "Ain't she something, Brian? Good thing she's so fine-looking or I wouldn't put up with that mouth for a minute."

Tia stands, picking up her book, her coffee, and a cinnamon roll. "Please excuse me," she says in a sincere voice of great falseness.

"Don't you want more breakfast than that?" Lisbon asks.

"Thank you for your concern," she says, again very sincerely, "but I'm having my very most favorite breakfast—major carbohydrates and a bucket of coffee. I know it's a misdemeanor, if not a felony, in this house not to subscribe to the four food groups, but I will be perfectly satisfied." She leaves the kitchen and I hear her bare feet going up uncarpeted stairs.

Lisbon shakes her head. "I swear, I don't know what is wrong with her. She's always been headstrong and sassy, but lately she has taken a turn for the worse."

"You got any help to offer, Brian?" Nathan asks. "You any kind of an expert on sixteen-year-old behavior?"

"I don't think so. Especially not girls."

"The funny part," Lisbon says, "is that her grades are as good as ever. She's top in her class, always has been, but her teachers these past six months or so say she's turned all smart-alecky and sullen and sometimes full-out rude. Just like she has at home."

"What happened six months ago?" I ask.

"Nothing that I know about. The only thing I can even think of is this story she wrote, she sent it to a magazine and she was so sure it was going to get published, but they didn't want it. I told her she should try somewhere else, or write another story, that she shouldn't give up so easy, that won't get you anywhere, but she wouldn't. Her pride was hurt, I guess, but she better get used to that if she's going to live in *this* world. And that's such a small thing, that couldn't be it. Maybe it's just growing pains. If it is, I hope it blows over soon. It's getting to be a real nuisance."

"It'd do her some good to be working with Rafe this summer," Nathan says. "Hard work can be a real friend."

"She must have other friends besides work," I say, thinking how much he sounds like Mom and how much I hate hearing that kind of advice. "Maybe they could help cheer her up." It's making me uncomfortable, talking about Tia. The fact that they're asking *my* opinion shows how worried they are, and what bad news this great-looking girl is.

"Actually, she's kept more to herself than ever lately," says Lisbon. "And she's never had a lot of friends." She looks right at me. "It's not so easy to be one of only a few black kids in school."

"I guess not," I say. I can't even imagine what it would be like. Then I wonder why she's in a school where she's so isolated. Why don't they live in a place with more black people if they want her to have black friends?

"Except for the boys," Nathan says, scowling. "They all want to be friends with her."

"Well, there's that," Lisbon says. "She's always been kind of like honey to bees. Boy bees. Even when she was little, the boys liked her. It's just gotten worse as she's gotten older. And that's a whole other set of problems. Hard to know what those white boys are wanting from her."

"Or black ones either," Nathan adds. "I used to be one of those and I know what they think about. Probably the same things white boys are thinking. At least some of the time."

He looks at me and I shrug. "My thoughts are all as pure as a baby's dreams," I say. Nathan and Lisbon laugh, but I feel they've deliberately drawn a line between us. Or maybe they're only making me look at differences that can't be denied.

"Well, does she have a boyfriend?" I ask. "Why don't you ask him what he thinks is wrong with her."

"One thing," Lisbon says, "there isn't just one boy, and another thing, I did ask a couple of them and they say they don't notice anything different. I guess she's always been on the haughty side with them."

I've had such a great morning, scubaing with Nathan,

and looking forward to a breakfast that has more than lived up to my expectations, but my feelings of well-being are leaking away. I can feel tension building in my shoulders.

"I'm going to go talk to her," Lisbon says.

"You think it'll do any good?" Nathan asks.

"I can't say," Lisbon says. "But she's mine and it's up to me to see that she knows what's the right way to be acting." She leaves the kitchen and I hear her feet on the stairs.

Nathan wipes his mouth with his napkin and pushes his chair back from the table. "Ah," he says. "I'm a happy man. That woman can cook."

"She sure can," I say. Suddenly I want to be back at Leo's, where the tension level is lower and more familiar.

"Tia's a worry to us now," he says. "Growing up can be a hard thing. Harder for some than others, that's the truth."

"I guess," I say.

"You scared of her?" he asks.

"Scared," I say, surprised. "Not scared, but she's not a lot of fun to be around. Why do you think I'm scared of her?"

"Oh, I didn't know if you were. But a lot of people are. She's smart and tough and she's got herself a mouth on her. A woman like that scares some men."

I hadn't thought of myself as a man or Tia as a woman.

"It's good you're not afraid of her," Nathan goes on.

Lisbon comes back into the kitchen.

"She okay?" Nathan asks.

Lisbon shrugs. "I did my talking. I don't know if she did her listening."

I'll bet my mother could have said the same words about me. And I get the feeling that Lisbon pushes on Tia as much as Mom does on me. It can get to be a real drag, especially the part about thinking whatever you do isn't good enough.

FIVE

Tia appears in shorts, T-shirt, and sandals, a stack of books under her arm and car keys in her hand. "Where's your grocery list?" she asks Lisbon.

Lisbon produces it and Tia sticks it in her pocket.

"What are your questions?" she asks Nathan.

He thinks for a minute and then says, "What's the southernmost state in the U.S. of A., and who won the Nobel Peace Prize in 1942?"

"Anything else?" she asks. No one says anything.

"Well," she says to me, "come on."

"Come on where?" I ask, startled.

"Marathon for errands," she says.

"But my clothes are wet," I say.

"Then we'll have to stop at your place, won't we?" she says and goes out the back door.

I look at Nathan and then at Lisbon. "Better get going," Nathan says.

I thank Lisbon for breakfast and follow Tia.

Tia keeps the motor running while I go into the cottage. Leo is gone. No note, no nothing, just gone. As usual. When I was younger, it scared me, the way he disappeared without any warning. But, eventually, I learned that he always came back, even if I never knew where he'd been.

I put on dry shorts, a fresh T-shirt, and running shoes and am ready to take off when I think of something.

I go to the kitchen and leave, prominently in the middle of the table, a note saying I'VE GONE TO MARATHON WITH TIA. I refuse to be like him. I will tell *him* where *I'm* going. I even add the time that I left.

When I get in the car, Tia says, "You remember those questions Nathan asked?"

"What's the southernmost state in the U.S. and who won the Nobel Peace Prize in 1942," I repeat. "Why?"

She doesn't answer, just drives with her bare left foot propped up on the hand brake, her left elbow on the open window, and the fingers of her right hand barely touching the steering wheel. Midway over the Seven Mile Bridge, at the highest point, she's going almost ninety.

"Hey," I say. "Slow down."

She gives me a sideways glance, taking her eyes off the road for what seems way too long to me. "So I'm in a hurry. Don't worry. I'm a good driver."

"I don't care how good you are," I say, "you need

33

some room for error and you don't have any. One twitch of that wheel and we're in the water."

"You can swim, can't you?"

"Only if I can get out of the car."

"That's why I leave the window open." She brakes hard as we come off the bridge into Marathon, and my seat belt almost strangles me. "See, we're there. You didn't have to worry."

She drives sedately through Marathon, which seems a town devoted to fish; the catching, eating, and contemplation of them. We stop at the library first and she quickly accumulates a pile of books while I browse. She hands me her books and says, "Time me."

She's back in eight minutes.

"What was I doing that for?" I ask her.

"I was looking up the answers to those questions. Remember those questions?"

"Sure. Southernmost state. Nobel Peace Prize. Well?"

"Hawaii and nobody. The world was at war in 1942. Nobody deserved it."

I'm impressed in spite of myself. I wouldn't know where to begin looking for those answers. "Why the questions?"

"Oh, it's one of Nathan's competitive things; his challenges. He gives me these assignments and thinks I won't be able to do them."

I see that Nathan pushes her, too, even though she's not his own child. And she can't resist the dare, in spite of resenting it at the same time, probably. I would.

"Sandra," she says to the clerk checking out her books, "my pal here needs a library card, okay? You can use my address for him."

"Sure," Sandra says. Sandra looks as if she should be modeling for swimsuit calendars instead of working in a library, but she efficiently makes me a perfectly useful library card. I don't mind having one, though I think Tia could have asked me first.

Then Tia thrusts two books at Sandra that she's put aside on the counter. "Here. Check these out for him."

"Hey, wait. You think I can't pick out my own books?"

"Just check them out for him, Sandra," she says. Turning to me, she says, "Don't worry. I'm not going to poison your impressionable mind with anything unseemly. You'll like these."

Sandra hands me the books, winks, and moves on to her next customer.

"*Red Sky at Morning,*" I say, reading the titles aloud. "*The Red Badge of Courage.* What is this, *red* week?"

"If you don't like them, then you can complain," she says as we walk out into the furnace of Marathon. "You trusted me with your life in the car. Don't tell me you won't trust me to choose your reading matter."

"I'll get back to you on that. Can we get something to drink?" I ask. "My mouth feels like I've been eating dog biscuits."

A fleeting expression passes across her face, something akin to humor, I think, but she doesn't actually smile. "Sure," she says. "There's a Quick-Mart near here. We could even walk if anybody was crazy enough to do that in this heat."

"Let's walk," I say. She shrugs and comes with me. I live in a city with good public transportation; Mom doesn't let me drive her car because she uses it for business, and I'm used to walking. I like knowing I can get places under my own power. Besides, I'm in no hurry to get back in a car with her.

"Hey, Tia," the clerk at the Quick-Mart says as we come in out of the glare into the cool store. He's big and blond and tan, about seventeen.

"Tom," she says, barely giving him a glance.

"So what are you doing for the summer?" he asks, leaning across the counter.

"Not much," she says, examining bottles in the cooler.

"I've been wanting to give you a call," he says.

"Hmm," she said, selecting apple juice.

I pay for my drink. Tom gives me my change and a look I interpret as hostile. I take the change, ignore the look, and wait by the door for Tia. She drops a cascade of coins onto the counter. "That's the right change," she says and walks away while he scrambles to count it.

"I'll be calling you," he says as Tia pushes open the door and goes out. I follow.

The quart bottle of Gatorade I guzzle down barely touches my thirst. I know I've sweated at least a quart since we left the library. I toss the bottle into the trash and watch Tia drink her apple juice in ladylike sips. The way it gleams wetly on her lower lip makes me want to touch her there. I've never felt that impulse before, and it makes me nervous.

"Where's your father?" I ask to distract myself.

She shrugs. "Gone, goner, gonest. He disappeared when my parents got divorced when I was five."

"You haven't seen him since then?"

"Nope. And I don't want to. Why should I?"

"Curiosity?"

"The fact that he disappeared tells me everything I want to know about him. Fathers only have one purpose anyway, and now that can be done in a laboratory. Men really are superfluous."

"I don't think so."

"Okay," she says. "Forget for a moment that you are one. What are they for, other than depositing their seed?"

I can feel myself getting red. My embarrassment must be the reason I can't think of a good answer. "Uh . . ." I say.

"Exactly," she responds. "Whereas women carry life and nurture it. They do the hard and dirty work of raising children. Often by themselves. They keep each other company and can be intimate on a deep emotional level, not that superficial physical thing that men like to call intimacy. And they can do anything else a man can do plus these things men can't do. So what are men for, answer me that?"

There must be something, but right now I can't think what it is.

"Well," she says, "you think about it and let me know if anything comes to mind. Let's go. I've got to get Mama's groceries."

She drops me off at Leo's feeling hot, hungry, and superfluous. I make myself two huge peanut butter, jelly, and mayonnaise sandwiches, drink what seems like a gallon of water, take a shower, and fall asleep in my undershorts on my bed.

The sound of the back door slamming wakes me. I'm hot and groggy and stiff from sleeping for a long time in the same position.

Leo opens the door to my room and leans in. "Takes a while to get used to the heat," he says. "You okay?"

"Yeah," I croak. I clear my throat. "I'm fine."

"I just wanted to let you know I'll be out this evening, but you can find something to eat, I guess."

"Sure." So he's not going to Lisbon's or he'd know I was going, too. I wonder if my leaving him a note this morning is the reason that, for once, he's remembering to tell me he's going out, even if not where.

He stands there for a minute, as if waiting for something. Then he says, "Okay," and backs out, rapping his knuckles once on the doorframe and leaving the door open.

Maybe Tia has a point, at least about fathers. What are they for?

SIX

I wait until I hear Leo go out again before I dress in clean shorts and a plaid shirt and try to tame my cowlick. I've forgotten how much laundry this climate creates with all the clothes-changing. It'll be a great labor saver if Dr. Ryker hires me and I can live in swim trunks and scuba gear.

When I get to the End of the Rainbow, Nathan is on the front porch with a man who must be Dr. Ryker, and Tia sits on the porch steps reading. She doesn't even look up as I approach. The citronella candles are lit and the bug zapper is working overtime, so the flying teeth are at a manageable level and, in the shade, the evening is better than tolerable; it's soft and plush-feeling.

It's hard to tell how tall Dr. Ryker is because he's sitting, but he looks to be about thirty-five and as if he's been dressed by three or four different people. Maybe

blind people. His shorts are plaid, his shirt wildly flowered, his sneakers scuffed, and his socks blue, though
not both the same blue. His hair and beard are sandy-
colored and appear to have been groomed with an egg-
beater. Somehow I expected something completely
different—someone careful, neat, precise, oriented to
fastidiously picking tiny archaeological things out of
sand and water.

"Hello, Brian," Nathan calls. "Come up here and
meet Rafe Ryker."

Dr. Ryker stands then, his hand out to me, and I can
see that he's over six feet tall and as muscular as a full-
back, though his handshake is surprisingly gentle.

"Call me Rafe," he says. "I hear you're a diver."

"I'm not very experienced, but I like it."

"That's half the battle," he says. "Everything else can
be learned if you've got a teacher who knows what he's
doing."

"Lucky for him he's got me," Nathan says, and
laughs.

"I'd guess he is lucky," Rafe says, sitting back down.

"I taught Tia," Nathan says, "and you've seen her.
She's good and she's careful."

Tia, without looking up from her book, actually almost smiles. When she does that, a dimple appears at
the corner of her mouth.

"I'm hiring only local divers," Rafe says. "It cuts costs.
But underwater archaeology is very specialized. Anybody who works for me will have to do it my way, and
that's a way many divers find tedious, especially those
who are only interested in uncovering some treasure."

Is that a job offer, I wonder, or just a comment.

"You interested?" Rafe asks.

"Sure," I say. "Yeah."

Tia is watching now, her book still open in her lap.

"You think you can you do it my way?" he asks.

"Why not?" I say.

He leans forward, his elbows on his knees. The last of the slanting sun catches in the hairs of his beard and on his forearms and calves, so that he looks almost gilded.

"An intact shipwreck is a time capsule," he says. "Everything in it is of a specific moment. The placement of the artifacts can tell us in what order the goods were loaded, where in the ship they were placed, what kinds of things various classes of passengers had in their personal baggage, how much smuggling went on, more information than you would believe. Every item has to be labeled and photographed and measured and recorded on to-scale graphs. Serious treasure hunters just want to get the stuff out of the way so they can find the jewels or the coins. I don't want anybody who thinks like that working for me."

"I don't think like that," I say.

"I can't pay very well," Rafe says.

"Like what?" I ask. It turns out to be more than minimum wage. "That's fine," I say.

Dr. Ryker nods. "I need good, enthusiastic divers and I'm not very well financed. One of the grants I was counting on fell through. Ideally, I'd like six divers, but I'm going to have to make do with four. I lost the two grad students who were going to help me—they got romantic and gave each other mononucleosis and now they both have to take it easy all summer." He looks at Tia. "Last chance," he says. "I've got a couple other people interested."

41

She lifts one shoulder. "Okay," she says. "Might as well."

From the corner of my eye I see Nathan's head turn toward her in surprise.

"Deal," Rafe says and goes on. "Most of my colleagues think I'm on a wild-goose chase, you know. They think the *Nueva Cádiz* sank farther down the Keys, closer to Key West."

"Then what makes you think it's here?" I ask.

He taps his heart with two fingers. "I know it here. And also because I went to Spain, to Seville, to the Archive of the Indies, and looked at original documents dealing with the Spanish conquest of the Americas. After I learned to read archaic Spanish, which is what they're written in. After I plowed through a good percentage of the fifty million things stored there."

"But what did you find that made you sure the *Cádiz* is here when nobody else thinks so?" I ask. I have an image of this big shaggy man rummaging in the Archive of the Indies, tossing piles of papers over his shoulders as slim, mustachioed Spaniards watch in horror.

"I got into some documents that had never been opened before. They were sent to Spain from Cuba at the turn of the century and just got piled up in the archive with a lot of other piled-up, uncatalogued documents. It's a scholar's nightmare in there. They tie the documents up in bundles—there can be five or ten thousand handwritten items in a bundle, in no order whatsoever. There's supposed to be a letter from Cortés to the King of Spain in there somewhere describing the conquest of Mexico. People have been looking for it for hundreds of years and haven't found it yet. That's why it's so amazing that anybody ever locates anything at all. There's a lot of luck or guardian angels or something involved. And that's what I had. I opened one of those Cuban bundles and there was a description of the wreck of the *Cádiz* by a contemporary sailor, a survivor of the wreck, with a crude map. It's not very accurate, but the way I read it, the *Cádiz* is less than a mile off Mosquito Key."

"Like I always say," Nathan says, "the harder you work, the luckier you get. But hasn't the shape of the Keys changed since the *Cádiz* sank? Seems like hurricanes are rearranging us all the time."

"That's true," Rafe says. "Shorelines change, islands come and go, measurements of miles and leagues are inconsistent. In those days, a fathom was the distance between the outstretched hands of the seaman hauling in the sounding lead line, so it could be anything from five to six and a half feet. Even place-names change. I learned from the map I found that Mosquito Key was once called Cayo del Marqués. The problem is, there were several other Cayos del Marqués then, too. And there are still some, though now they're called the Marquesas, west of Key West, which is where everybody else thinks the *Cádiz* is. And where it actually might be, no matter what I think. Or feel in my heart. Or it could be completely buried in sand or completely disintegrated. Would you want to invest money in an operation like that?"

"Pretty high flying, all right," Nathan says. "But if you find it, the payoff's good. And you did find the *Buen Viaje.*"

"That was a lot easier. Others had located it before and then lost it again. I knew pretty closely where to look, and I had a pile more money. This is a lot more of a crap shoot. But you're right, the payoff would be excellent. An unsalvaged ship from 1648 could tell us so much about that time."

"Not to mention the King's treasure," Tia says.

"Not to mention that. Nothing attracts as much attention as gold and silver, even though that's not the most interesting part to an archaeologist. But it's helpful to have some treasure to auction off to finance the rest of the salvage operation."

"Do you really think we could find it?" I ask.

"I wouldn't be here if I didn't think that," he says.

Lisbon comes through the door to the porch. "Supper's ready. Come on in, y'all."

We gather around the lace-covered table in the high-ceilinged dining room. A fan turns languidly above us. Lisbon sits at the head of the table with Tia on one side of her and Nathan on the other. I sit next to Tia, and Rafe is next to Nathan. Lisbon clasps hands with Tia and Nathan. After a momentary hesitation, Tia takes my hand, while Nathan takes Rafe's. Rafe reaches across the table to take my other hand, but I'm concentrating on Tia's strong, cool hand on mine.

Lisbon lowers her head and begins a prayer unlike any I, who have spent almost no time inside a church, have ever heard.

"Well, Lord, we're all here, about to take part in Your bounty, and we want to thank You for just about everything. I'm thankful to have my daughter and my good man at my table, and to have two fine guests. My business is doing well now, and I thank You for that. Weather's not too bad, either, for this time of year. I know You'll be watching over this hunt for Dr. Rafe's ship, and if it's meant to be found, well, then he'll find it.

44

Amen." After a pause, she added, "Anybody else who wants to add something can do that now."

There is a moment of quiet and then Nathan says, "I'm a happy man today, and I know You had something to do with it. Thanks."

Another pause lengthens. I try to think of something to say.

Rafe clears his throat. "I ask for Your guidance with my search." He clears his throat again.

All the heads remain bowed, and I know I have to say something. I've never thought about praying in this chatty fashion and am having a hard time escaping from my preconceptions of what prayers should sound like: formal and solemn, always ending with "Amen." Not to mention that I'm wondering if there's really anybody listening. "I—" My voice cracks. I start over. "I . . . I'm glad to be here and I hope the rest of my stay is as good. Thank You."

It isn't much of a prayer, but maybe you only get good at it if you do it a lot. Anyway, it's true; I am having a good time.

Quickly, Tia says, "I pass," and we release each other's hands and raise our heads. I feel the phantom print of Tia's fingers on mine all through the meal.

Lisbon is as wonderful a cook for dinner as she was for breakfast. Almost everything is something new to me and delicious—shredded pork and fried platanos, frijoles negros and spicy rice, pompano fixed so that even I like it. I eat like a starving lumberjack.

"There's homemade peach ice cream for dessert," Lisbon says, "but I think we should set a spell first, let the other things settle down."

"I couldn't eat any more right now to save my very

4 5

life," Nathan says. "I'm not even sure I can make it to the porch to set a spell."

"I'll help you, old man," Lisbon says. "Give me your arm, you sorry thing."

Arm in arm they lead us out to the porch again, and we find places to watch the lavender-streaked sky settle into darkness. Tia and I sit opposite each other halfway down the steps, leaning against the balusters.

The indigo evening flows over us, pooling into shadows in the corners of the porch. The light from the dining room makes a pale stripe across the floorboards. The citronella candles flicker on the railing while Nathan, Lisbon, and Rafe talk quietly behind us, and a bird makes a strange sound in a strange tree in Lisbon's yard.

"Plover," Tia says, "in the gumbo-limbo tree. They sound so sad."

"The what tree?" I ask.

"Gumbo-limbo. Also known as the tourist tree because the peeling red bark looks like a sunburn. Are you sure you've been coming to Florida every summer? You don't know anything about the Keys."

"I never stayed very long. A couple of weeks at the most. And Leo moves around—all over Florida, not just the Keys. This is the first time I've come to the same place two summers in a row. I don't do much while I'm here. Usually my dad goes out fishing and I stay in."

"Why don't you go out with him?"

"When I was younger and couldn't be left alone, I did. But I used to get seasick a lot, which made me a nuisance. I don't do that anymore, I'm relieved to say, but I still don't think fishing for days at a time is the most fun. Well, once I might have gotten sick from watching these guys my dad was fishing with kill a shark. You'd have thought they'd caught a vampire or a werewolf or something, the way they clubbed it and cut it open and broke out its teeth, while they slid around in the gore. I know everybody's afraid of sharks, but this was primitive. Sharks just do what sharks are supposed to do; it's not calculated.''

"Not calculated, huh?"

She's making me feel not only *superfluous* but stupid, and it's making me mad.

"Well, how would you say it?" I ask hotly.

"I was admiring your description, not criticizing. You don't have to get so testy."

"You don't exactly make conversation easy, you know. It's actually a pretty big pain to try to talk to somebody who makes such a production of being so aloof and superior. If I didn't know you were a woman, and therefore better than us poor dumb unnecessary men, I'd say you were miserable and angry about something. That makes testy pretty small-time, if you ask me."

Without a word, she stands up and goes into the house.

Lisbon stops talking in the middle of a sentence and watches her go. Nathan jumps in to finish Lisbon's sentence, while Rafe looks confused.

I come up the steps and take a chair on the porch. I haven't had dessert yet, and I'm not going to miss Lisbon's peach ice cream.

SEVEN

Leo's still out when I get home. I lie uncovered on my bed listening to the air conditioner labor, and wonder what the heat will be like by the end of my stay. Always before, I've served my time in Florida as soon as school lets out and been home by the Fourth of July. Now the summer stretches ahead on Mosquito Key. And, oddly, I don't mind, the way I always have before. I'm going to be in on a treasure hunt. I'm going to get to be a great scuba diver. And something is going on with me and Tia that's a mystery but interesting.

I wake early when the sun comes in past the shade I've forgotten to lower. I shuffle into the kitchen and am surprised to find Leo there sitting at the table, the dirty dishes pushed aside, with a cup of instant coffee in front of him and a cigarette burning in an overflowing ashtray.

"Hey," he says, his voice gravelly. "You're up early."

"I guess." I pour myself a glass of orange juice. "You coming in or going out?"

He raises his head and laughs, a short, sharp bark. "Both. I've got one last load of tourists to take out fishing today before I start in on the treasure hunt."

"I'm going to be working on the hunt, too."

"Yeah? Rafe took you on?" He squints his eyes against the smoke from his cigarette as he inhales deeply.

"Yeah." I don't like hearing the surprise in his voice.

"When did you meet him?"

"Last night." I don't need to give him all the details. Why should I? He doesn't tell me anything about his apparently active social life.

"You think you're ready for that?" His tone seems to makes it clear what he thinks.

"Maybe not completely," I say. My throat hurts from the effort of keeping my voice calm. "But I will be. And Nathan says he'll teach me."

"Ryker must be more desperate for divers than I thought." He takes a drag of his cigarette and blows the smoke out fast. I relax my grip on the juice glass before I find myself with a handful of shards.

"Tia's going to work for him, too."

"That's different. She's been diving for years, with Nathan. There's nobody better than Nathan."

"Get used to it, Leo." I mean to put my empty juice glass down on the counter softly, but I slam it.

"Hey. Take it easy," Leo say. "What's the problem?"

"No problem. I've got to go."

I shove my feet into my flip-flops and leave, banging

the door behind me. I have no idea where I'm headed.

I end up at Nathan's dock, sweating more than the humidity justifies.

"Good morning, Brian," Nathan calls from the deck of the *Angelfish*, where he leans with a cup of coffee in his hand. "Seems like you got a burr under your saddle. What's going on?"

"Nothing."

"Yeah, I know all about those nothings. They always mean *something*." He drinks some coffee while I stand on the dock looking at my feet. "They always mean something you think talking about won't help," he says, "but sometimes it does. And just so you know, I got two good ears and a mouth I know how to keep shut. I can listen."

"Okay," I say, still examining my feet.

Nathan takes a deep breath. "Well, you interested in a little before-breakfast dive?"

We stay in the water longer than the day before, practicing clearing our face masks, buddy breathing, and emergency ascents, blowing bubbles all the way up so our lungs won't rupture. With Nathan beside me, the first few breaths don't scare me anymore, the way they used to.

The calm, methodical, almost effortless diving with Nathan is the perfect antidote to being with Leo, like a vacation on another planet. And underwater *is* another planet, just as Nathan promised, where even the medium we move in is different. And the light and the inhabitants. Being a fish might not be so bad: food seems plentiful, there's lots of companionship that requires nothing that I can see in the way of communication, and the fact of being cold-blooded relieves you of having to feel any annoying emotions.

"We won't be diving any deeper than thirty or so feet looking for the *Cádiz*," Nathan says as we sit on the dock taking off our gear, cleaning and drying it and checking it out before stowing it away, "and at that depth you won't have to worry about decompression, but I need to be sure you know how to look up the tables for it, right?"

"Yeah," I say. "I had good instruction. I just didn't like diving in Lake Michigan the way I do here."

"That's good." He puts his hand on my shoulder. "You hungry yet? Personally, I could eat this dock without even syrup."

"Yeah, I'm hungry. Leo's gone out with a fishing party. You want to come back to our place for breakfast? It's kind of a mess, but there's food."

"I've seen Leo's mess, thank you, and that's not the setting I want for my hard-earned breakfast." He stands and pulls on shorts and then a T-shirt. "Come on. I'll buy you breakfast at Captain Hook's. We can't keep making a nuisance of ourselves with Lisbon. She's got her own work to do."

We sit at the counter at Captain Hook's, where PeeWee waits on us again. She doesn't seem in any better mood than she was a couple of nights ago.

"Don't you ever go home, PeeWee?" Nathan asks.

"Not in the slow season. I need the money." She slaps setups down in front of us. "You know what you want?"

"You got a smile in there anywhere?" Nathan asks.

51

She gives him a feeble imitation of one. "That's the best I can do under the circumstances."

"And what about those circumstances?" he asks. "Man trouble?"

She nods. "The usual."

"Get yourself a new man, that's what I say, if the old one don't work so good."

"I'm sure that's excellent advice," she says, pouring each of us a cup of coffee without asking if we want one. "I can't decide if I'm an optimist or an idiot to keep hoping for a change."

"You're going to need a better smile than that one you gave us if you do go looking for a new man," Nathan tells her, and takes a sip of his coffee.

This time her smile is real. "You're right again."

"Ah, that's better. Now you can bring us some bacon and eggs and hotcakes so we can smile, too."

When she's gone, with my eyes on my coffee cup I ask, "Is Leo the man who's giving her trouble?"

"They spend time together," Nathan says carefully.

"You gave her good advice, then." I take a sip of the coffee.

"You having troubles with the man, too?"

"No more than usual." I put the cup back in its saucer.

"You don't see much of your dad, huh? Well, I never even knew mine. It leaves a hole, there's no doubt about that. But it's a hole that can be filled, I learned. You just got to watch what you fill it with."

"What did you fill yours with?" I've never noticed a hole left by Leo's absence. He leaves barely a dent on me. Tia seems to feel the same way about her father. Maybe Nathan doesn't have this right.

"The wrong things for a long time, so I know what I'm talking about. Trouble, women, substances. Then I just got worn out with that stuff and I wanted to find myself a chance. I joined the Navy; worked hard, earned some respect—from myself, too, and high time—and got myself straight. I don't know your daddy too well, but he did tell me he was glad you were coming."

"Right," I say.

Nathan gives me a long look. "Could be true," he says. "Not everybody's good at showing what they feel. Or even at *knowing* what they feel. Anyway, I'd say the person you most need to worry about impressing is yourself."

"Maybe," I say. "I've sure never impressed Leo."

Nathan turns and looks at me. "Well, you impress me with the way you go at learning to scuba. You impressed Rafe enough to hire you for the treasure hunt."

"He's just desperate for cheap labor," I put in, repeating Leo's opinion.

"The hell he is. You think a man like him is going to take on somebody who might mess up his whole careful operation? You wouldn't think he cares so much if you go by the way he looks, but he does. He believes you'll do things his way. You might even have impressed Miss Tia."

"Yeah, right," I say. "Do you know she thinks men are useless?"

"She been giving you that mess, too? She's just all angry and looking for a place to put it. Men seem like a good spot. Not just white men, either. All of us. Certain ways, though not many, I guess color makes no difference."

It occurs to me that Nathan and Lisbon think about

what color they are a lot more than I do. Maybe it's hard to avoid if you're any color besides white.

When PeeWee brings our breakfasts, she bats her eyelashes at Nathan. "How's this?" she asks. "Does it make your blood heat up?"

"Absolutely," Nathan says. "But don't try it on me anymore. I don't want to get in trouble with Lisbon."

"I don't believe there's any way anybody could lure you away from Lisbon," PeeWee says. "Say, what about that big guy with the beard that's staying at her place?"

"That's Dr. Raphael Ryker. He's looking for the *Nueva Cádiz*. He'll probably spend most of his time out on the water this summer, but I'll steer him in here if you're interested."

"I'm interested. In anybody. You can send some of those other treasure hunters in here as well."

"What other treasure hunters?" he asks.

She shrugs. "Some guys—two of them—were in here the other day. I think I overheard them talking about sunken treasure."

"That's interesting," he says thoughtfully.

"Oh, there's always somebody around thinking they'll find the answer to their prayers underwater." She picks up the coffeepot and goes to pour refills for the other customers at the counter. She's smiling.

After a minute of silence, Nathan says, "So what you going to do for the rest of the day?"

"I got some books at the library yesterday. I guess I'll read. Or maybe I'll go snorkeling if I can borrow some gear. Or take some pictures. I don't know."

"So you're a photographer?"

I shrug. "Yeah, I guess. I like it. I want to get better, try new things."

"That's good," he says. "Sure you can borrow some gear. But no snorkeling alone, you know that. Why don't you see if Tia wants to go along? She can show you some good places. More interesting than here."

"I don't know if I'm up to another round with her."

"Just a suggestion."

"I thought everybody who lives in the Keys is supposed to be real laid-back."

"Well, she was born down here, but she didn't come laid-back. Some folks just got more push and starch to them than others."

"She's got that, all right."

"That something you like?"

I think about it. My mother has plenty of push and starch and I don't always like it, especially not the part of it that's directed at me. And I'm not sure I like it in Tia, though it does make her different from any girl I know. I wonder if my mother seemed that way to Leo once.

"Sometimes," I finally say. "I don't like it so much in my mother."

"You might if she wasn't your mother."

"Maybe."

Nathan wipes his mouth and finishes the last swallow of his coffee. "I got to go meet the Doc. We're going out in the *Angelfish* to check out the lease sites. You want to go over to Lisbon's with me? See what Miss Tia's got on her mind for today?"

"Okay," I say. But only because snorkeling with somebody, even if it's Tia, sounds better to me than spending the day alone.

EIGHT

I feel pretty good walking to the End of the Rainbow with Nathan. My legs are sore from two days of kicking with flippers, but sore means I'm building muscle. I'm full of a big breakfast, in the company of an unusual man, and on my way to see a complicated girl who thinks I'm useless.

Tia sits in the shade on the porch, her bare legs slung over the arm of a wicker chair, a thick book in her lap. When she sees Nathan and me coming up the walk, she straightens but doesn't take off her dark glasses, and doesn't say anything.

"Hey, Miss Tia," Nathan says. "How you doing?"

"Okay," she says, holding her finger inside the closed book to keep her place.

"I'm here to collect the Doc and get out on the bounding main." He goes up the steps and opens the screen door. "You two play nice, now, you hear?"

When he's gone inside, Tia opens her book again and begins to read.

"What are you reading?" I ask.

"Carl Sagan," she says without looking up.

"What about Carl Sagan?" I'm not going to let her off that easily.

She looks up and, speaking in her sincere voice, says, "He's convinced there's life on other planets and that there's a way for us to get in contact. What do you think?"

"I don't know. I never thought about it." Interesting that she's reading about communication with space people and not with earth people. "Possible, I suppose. There's a lot of planets. It's a little arrogant of us to think we're the only life around. Or that we're even the smartest ones around."

"And do you think senses of humor exist on other planets?" she asks sincerely.

"Only on inhabited ones," I say.

She gets that look again, like she wants to smile but won't let herself. She slumps back in the chair and acts as if she's reading.

"You want to go snorkeling? Nathan says I can't go alone. He also said you know some good places."

She looks up but doesn't close her book. "I do," she says.

"So do you want to go or not?"

"Why should I?"

"It would be hospitable to a visitor? It would be fun?" I want to go snorkeling, so I give her a way to come with me. "You could try to drown me?"

"I'll take that one. I think you've asked for it."

"You're probably right." I'm a little embarrassed

about my—what did she call it?—testiness last night. Even though I believe what I said to her, maybe I didn't need to be quite so direct. But she'd made me mad. This morning, however, I've got a stomachful of pancakes and cholesterol and a head full of underwater light. I feel good. I want her to show me a great snorkeling place. And I can't go without her.

She shrugs and shuts the book. "Okay. Come get me in half an hour."

It takes me half an hour to collect the snorkeling gear from Nathan's dock, stop by the cottage to pick up a camera and my running shoes, and return to the End of the Rainbow.

Tia is waiting on the porch. There are two bikes on the walk, one with a large beach bag in the basket. Her curly hair is in a ponytail stuck through the opening in the back of her baseball cap, and she wears white shorts and a pink T-shirt that give her brown skin a rosy glow. She looks like an advertisement for vitamins that make you sullen. When I pull out my camera, she turns away, but I take the shot anyway.

Bahia Honda State Park has a real beach, long and white, with palm trees growing in the sand and picnic tables. And it's deserted except for a pregnant woman with two preschoolers paddling in the water. She lets me take some pictures of them. Somehow, Florida has become an interesting place to photograph again.

The snorkeling by the bridge piers is great: colorful fish, lobsters, sponges, and fantastic coral formations. I feel as if I consist only of a big eye, yet still not big enough to see everything I want to see. Tia finds the best things, the basket sponges, the star corals, and the tropical fish with dots and stripes and bands of color. She pokes me and points and leads me to things to see. She doesn't try to drown me. Underwater, she is a different person: generous, curious, cooperative. Maybe speech has been an evolutionary mistake; maybe everybody would get along better if we couldn't talk to each other.

When eventually we get tired and make our way back to the shore, I'm in a nearly mesmerized state from the display of fantastic life and color that shows not at all if you only stand on the beach and look at the water.

"That's nothing compared to the reefs," Tia says as we come out of the water. "They're unbelievable. Fish love reefs. They like wrecks, too. Plain empty water doesn't offer the food supply that a reef or a wreck does."

"I'd like to learn how to take pictures underwater," I say, the idea coming to me from my still-submerged mind. "I know how to do it on land, but it's so different down there."

"I think Nathan's got an underwater camera somewhere. He went through a spell of photography. But the strange thing was, the pictures, even though they were beautiful, weren't very interesting. They looked like picture postcards, ones you've seen a million times. He decided plain old beauty isn't always what's interesting. You've got to show something else besides the beauty, something behind it—he called it the 'meat.' And he could never figure out how to do that."

"I could." I've already done it, sometimes, with my

photographic experiments. I can't say how I know, but there are times when I look through the lens that I just *know* I've got a face or a scene or a composition that's more than what it shows; that's somehow a story. I've already learned that the camera *does* lie; that you can get more, or less, than what you think you're going to get; that the lens doesn't see everything. The brain behind the lens makes a difference.

Tia looks at me. "What makes you think so?"

"I don't know for sure. I just think I could. I've done a lot of photography—I have a darkroom at home. But underwater's so different—the light, the shapes, the . . . the mystery. It seems like it's almost *demanding* that I take pictures. And I know I could find some meanings, some . . . something more."

She looks at me curiously. "What does that mean?"

I struggle to think how to explain it and finally have to say, "I can't put it into words. It's a feeling."

She's quiet for a moment. "You know those little purple fish, the wrasses, the really, really purple ones?"

"Yeah, what about them?"

"They're so purple it goes all the way through. Their bones are even blue."

"Yes," I say. "That's what I would show. How what's on the outside affects what's on the inside. Or maybe it's the other way around. Or both." I feel as if my eyes are turned inward. I'm aware that Tia is taking a paper sack out of her beach bag and opening it on the picnic table in front of me, but I am focused somewhere else. It doesn't even occur to me to be surprised that she's made a lunch for us. And not just any lunch, but a gourmet one: cream cheese, olive, and sun-dried-tomato sandwiches; green grapes; iced tea; and fancy cookies. I, who am used to giant PB, jelly, and mayo lunches, watch myself and try not to do anything uncouth while I eat.

We finish our lunch in silence and then lie on our beach towels in the shade. Tia falls asleep in a few minutes, but I lie, eyes open but unfocused, constructing images of things I haven't even seen yet.

Tia wakes suddenly and digs in her beach bag for her watch. "I've got to go," she says.

"Do you have to be somewhere?"

She rolls over and closes her eyes against the glare. "Yeah."

I wait but she doesn't elaborate. I get to my feet and begin folding my towel.

"Thank you," she says quietly.

I stop folding. "For what?"

Not looking at me, she collects her things.

"You mean for the snorkeling?" I ask.

She doesn't answer, but piles her things in her basket and gets on her bicycle. I follow her the three miles to Mosquito Key, as hooked and baffled as any marlin.

NINE

I'm flat on my back, dead asleep, with the door to my room open when Leo comes in from his day on the fishing boat. The slam of the kitchen door wakes me as it did the day before.

"Hey," Leo says, pausing in the doorway. "You okay?"

"Sure," I say, sitting up.

"I saw the *Angelfish* out there this afternoon."

"Yeah? Nathan told me they were going out. What were they doing?"

"All the technical stuff to get ready for the search. Just don't ask me what it is. I haven't a clue."

I can't think of anything to say. Leo stands in the doorway as if he's waiting for something, but I don't know what it is.

Finally he says, "You okay for dinner?"

I don't know what that means. Do I have plans for

dinner? Can I fix myself some dinner? Does he want to have dinner with me? Do I want dinner at all? I nod. "Yeah. Sure," I say, having no idea what I'm agreeing to.

"Okay, then," he says, and raps on the doorframe with his knuckles before he goes on down the hall. Soon I hear the shower. I'm dressed and channel-surfing in the living room when Leo comes out of his room in clean khaki shorts and one of his flowered shirts. His hair is wet and combed so neatly it looks as if he's used surveying tools.

He puts his hand out and for a minute I think he's going to touch me, but he lets it fall onto the arm of my recliner. "So you're okay for dinner," he says again.

"Yeah."

"Okay. Well, another time, then," he says and goes through the kitchen and out the door.

It's only after he's gone that I work out what he'd been saying. He was asking me to have dinner with him. And then somehow thinking I had something else to do.

I shake my head. I need a code book to decipher the smallest conversation with him.

I decide to head over to the End of the Rainbow after I have something to eat and see if Nathan is there. Nathan will know about the technical stuff and, better still, he'll know how to talk to me about it.

Nathan isn't there. Neither is Tia. But Lisbon gives me a slice of Key lime pie and a glass of iced tea while she cleans up the kitchen.

"You finish that and then you can go on over to Nathan's," she says.

"To Nathan's?" I ask, my mouth full of pie. "I

thought, I mean, the way he comes in and out of here, I thought . . .''

She hangs the dish towel up to dry and smiles at me. "No, Nathan doesn't live here."

"I'm sorry," I say, embarrassed. "I didn't mean to insult you or anything."

She puts her hand on my head gently, almost as if she is giving me a blessing. "For you to think that I'm living with the finest man I've ever known is no insult to me, Brian. And Nathan and I are as bound to each other as it's possible for two people to be, but we don't live together. Somehow, living apart is one of the things that lets us be close. I know it's hard to understand, but that's how it works best for us. And, we hope, for Tia. She's always part of our thoughts." She takes her hand off my head. "I left the Keys for about three years after Tia's dad took off. Trying to run away from the heartache, I suppose, but it was a mistake. One of the reasons I came back to Mosquito Key was to get her away from some bad influences. I wanted her to be safe and happy, and now sometimes I think I've isolated her too much. So I'm grateful for Nathan."

"Tia," I say, without thinking. I like the sound of her name. Then I think that no adult has ever been that honest with me before.

She sighs and nods. "Tia," she repeats. "She's his, too, in every way but blood." She goes back to wiping the counter with a sponge.

I suddenly want that so much I can't swallow, a man to be that kind of father to me, the way Nathan is to Tia. Someone whose thoughts I'm always in, who thinks about how each of his choices and decisions will affect me, who believes that he is as bound to me as a person can be. No wonder Tia doesn't miss her father. She has Nathan.

This news shocks and frightens me, and I try to push it back into a crevice of my mind. It has no connection to how it is with Leo and me. But now I know Nathan is right: not having a father does leave a hole.

"Your daddy, now, he's different from Nathan," she says, as if she's read my mind. "He's not so steady. He could be—most anybody can be—but he hasn't figured out how yet."

I lick my fork and put it down. "Can you tell me how to find Nathan?"

She gives me directions and sees me to the front door. Just before I open it, I thank her for the pie and she says, "You're not like your daddy, you know."

Nathan lives in a two-room cabin up on stilts that looks like nothing else on Mosquito Key: one big room over the other, with the bathroom over the kitchen and an elegant narrow brass spiral staircase connecting the two floors. "Built it myself," he says. "I like having the sleeping part separate from the living part. And lining up the plumbing made it easier to build. It's not for everybody, but I like it."

"So do I," I say.

The walls are teak, warm and brown, like the stateroom of a luxury liner, and everywhere are artifacts of the sea: brass instruments atop the old seaman's trunk that serves as a coffee table, seashells lined along the windowsills, color photographs of fish and coral, and, in a wide shell on the trunk, a corroded, oxidized belt buckle.

"What's that?" I ask, pointing to it.

"That's one of the reasons I think Rafe knows what he's talking about. I've brought up a lot of things in fishing nets over the years that have to be from a shipwreck: cannonballs, buckles, utensils, some silver coins from the early 1600s. I know it's out there."

"That's what I came to ask you about. How are we going to find it? Do we just dive every day and look around?"

"Won't be much diving for a while. First we'll sweep the areas he's got the leases on—you have to lease search sites from the state of Florida, you know—with a magnetometer. That picks up on concentrations of iron, like cannon or anchors. That's what we did today: set out the markers for the sweep. Those ships all carried a lot of anchors—it was pretty easy to lose them, and you needed some spares—and a lot of cannon, too. If you can get close enough to the bottom—remember now, this ship could be buried in ten or twenty feet of sand—you can pick up readings from little stuff, like buttons, spoons, fittings. When we get a concentration of hits, then we go down and have a look, suction off some sand and see what's there. Sometimes ships break up when they sink, especially during a storm, and they spread out all over the place. The *Cádiz* went down because of negligence or accident, according to Rafe, not a storm, so she should be all in one place. She almost made it to shore, and some of the sailors did. One of them must have left the record of the sinking that the Doc found in the archive. That's the best record you can have, straight from somebody who knows what he's talking about."

"You make it sound like it'll be easy. If it is, why hasn't somebody else found her already?"

"Like the Doc says, they all think she's farther down the Keys. But I think she's here, close."

I feel a shiver along my spine at the idea of an intact ship, waiting through the long years, quiet and secret under tons of sand and water.

Then, remembering: "Tia said you had an underwater camera."

"Yeah, I got a Nikonos V around here somewhere. You interested in taking some pictures?"

"I'd like to try. How hard is it to do?"

"Not hard. You got to do all the same things you have to do with land photography—find a subject, compose your shot, make sure all the readings are okay, light ratios and that stuff—then hope your fish will stand still and smile for you."

"What about the light? Will it be as light underwater out where we're looking for the *Cádiz* as it is where you and I have been diving?"

"Light's good out there. Thirty feet is considered shallow, and the bottom is sand, so it reflects. It'll look like being inside Jell-O. The only thing you have to get used to is the distortion from the face-mask lens. It makes things look bigger. Remember that when you find some curious creature looking over your shoulder. It's not as big as you think."

"Great," I say. "I'll remember that."

"Let me go dig up that camera and I'll show you how it works."

We spend the rest of the evening with the camera and going through some books of underwater photography.

At ten-thirty I stand up to go.

Nathan hands me the camera. "You take this with you. I haven't used it in a coon's age. You can return it when you go back to Chicago." He pauses. "Rafe needs to have a photographic record of the search. He meant to take the pictures and develop them himself. Lisbon's let him set up a darkroom in one of her bathrooms. If you get good at this, you could save him a lot of time."

My hands fit around the camera as if they've been waiting for it all my life. "Thanks," I say. I can't think when I've meant that word more.

"You just get some great shots with it, son. And leave some of them with me when you go. Okay?"

"Sure." The weight of the camera seems just heavy enough to be an anchor for me.

TEN

All the way back to Leo's, I turn the camera in my hands, holding it up to my eye, focusing on the Shrimp Shack, the Silver Palms, the dock where the *Angelfish* and the *Crazy Conch* rest, the moon flirting through the palm fronds. I imagine piles of color photos, illustrations worthy of *National Geographic*; and piles of black-and-whites, compelling and thoughtful.

I come into the kitchen to hear Leo on the phone, yelling, "How far away can he be? Fortunata's a little place. For God's sake, Laura, he's almost seventeen . . . Okay, so he's sixteen. Give him some room."

Gently I close the door, but Leo hears me.

"Here he is, he's just come in, all in one piece." He holds the phone out to me.

"Mom?" I say into the mouthpiece. I haven't thought of her once in the past two days. "What time is it where you are? Where are you?"

I listen while she explains that it's almost five in the morning in Paris, but they have to catch an early plane to Rome, so she was up and thought it would be a good time to call me. Where had I been?

"Visiting," I say. "I've been scuba-diving."

"At night?" she cries. "What is Leo thinking of? That sounds crazy-dangerous. Put him back on."

"Not at night," I say. "I was visiting a guy I've been diving with. He loaned me an underwater camera."

"Camera?" she said. "You have a camera. Plus that fancy one, that Hasselblad or whatever it is that Bill gave you. Did you forget to pack them?"

"No, I have them. This is an underwater camera I'm talking about, Mom. Don't worry. Everything's fine."

She hesitates. "It is?"

"Yeah. Pretty much." I decide not to mention the hunt for the *Cádiz*. That would send her into orbit all over again.

"I worry about you wandering around after dark," she says.

"There's no reason to. Fortunata's three blocks long on a key that's not much bigger than that. What could happen?"

"I've heard those alligators walk down the middle of the streets, and coral snakes can hide anywhere. Not to mention there's a hurricane every five minutes."

"Mom, I've been coming to Florida for years and you know I've never seen any snakes or alligators except in tourist places or any hurricanes ever. Quit worrying." She always does this when I'm at Leo's, makes these semihysterical phone calls fussing about all kinds of improbable, exotic things.

"Why did he have to go to such a strange place? Why couldn't he have settled in some nice midwestern town?"

She says this every summer, but it wouldn't have mattered if he had. Then she'd be thinking about tornadoes or serial killers or rabid raccoons.

The only time I feel sorry for my mother is when I'm not with her, when all her latent maternal concerns go into hand-wringing overdrive. Once I'm back in Chicago, we'll take each other for granted again. Yet, as annoying as these phone calls are, I recognize that they're proof she's thinking about me even when I'm not right in front of her.

"Fortunata's fine. You'd better go. You'll miss your plane."

"Oh, my God, you're right. Are you sure you're okay?"

"I'm doing great. 'Bye, Mom. Have a good time." I hang up.

"You were at Nathan's?" Leo asks.

"Yeah. He loaned me his camera."

Leo picks up the camera and looks through the viewfinder. "Yeah, he got some good pictures with this. You say he loaned it to you?"

I'm angry in an instant. "What do you think, I stole it? Yeah, he loaned it to me. Ask him if you don't believe me."

"Hey. Watch your mouth. I'm still your father, even if you are as big as me."

"I'm bigger."

We stand facing each other. I'm taller, but Leo's heavier. My fists are clenched and my father grips the camera so hard I can see his knuckles are white. Then he relaxes his grip and hands the camera to me.

"I'm going to bed," he says and leaves. He closes the door to his room.

I stand there, holding on to the camera as if it's all that's keeping me up, and my hands are shaking. I was a second away from taking a punch at my own father.

Why couldn't we quit pretending there was any reason for them and call off these annual visits? Maybe this should be my last trip. He must have noticed how we both counted the seconds until I could leave.

The thought of never coming to Florida to see Leo again leaves me with a strange hollow feeling as if I'm very hungry, but too sick to eat.

ELEVEN

Leo stands at the counter making coffee, not instant but real coffee with grounds, in the pot. The sink is full of soapy water in which the accumulation of dishes soaks. The table is cleared and washed and there's a fresh plastic bag in the trash can.

"Morning," I say.

"Morning," Leo says. "Coffee?"

"Okay." I don't really want any, but I don't want to be difficult. It seems as though the vibrations from last night are still quivering in the air, like the echo of a guitar chord.

"You going out on the *Angelfish* or with me?" Leo asks.

"I didn't know you were going out, too. I already told Nathan I'd go with him."

"Okay," Leo says. "Maybe tomorrow."

"Yeah," I say, taking the coffee mug my father offers me. "Well, I better get dressed." I take my coffee back to my bedroom while I dress, then take it with me into the bathroom, where I empty it down the sink.

Leo's in his own room when I go through the kitchen on my way out. I stop long enough to clump some peanut butter on a couple of pieces of toast, which I eat while I walk to Nathan's.

I knock lightly on the edge of the screen door.

"Enter," Nathan calls.

The big living room is spotless. The photography books we'd been looking at the night before are neatly on the bookshelf, the glasses we'd drunk from are gone, the pillows on the couch are plumped.

"I'm in the kitchen," Nathan calls, even though I can see him from where I am.

He's drying his breakfast dishes and putting them away. Everything in the immaculate space is shipshape.

"Can I offer you something before we take off? Orange juice? Lemonade?"

"Either's fine," I say, my mouth cottony from wolfing the peanut butter on the run.

"Good idea to keep hydrated in this humidity. You can sweat a quart without hardly even trying."

"I've noticed," I say. I drink the juice, then rinse out the glass and set it in the sink. "Should I wash it before we go?" I ask.

"I'm not that compulsive," Nathan says. "It can wait. Everything is balance, son. What's important, what isn't. What needs your attention, what doesn't. It ain't easy 'cause it changes, but you got to think about it. I can leave a glass or two in the sink for a day, but I don't want to let them start piling up day after day—not that

I'm saying anything against your daddy, I want you to know that, because I know it doesn't bother him. But it bothers me. It means something to me about myself, about the kind of person I am, so I take care of it. You understand?"

I nod even though I'm not sure I do.

"That's good. I know you're the kind of kid who figures things out." He picks up the picnic cooler. "You ready?"

I follow him out. I'm the kind of kid who figures things out? What could make him think that? What does he think I should be figuring out?

Tia and Rafe are already on board the *Angelfish* when Nathan and I arrive. Tia seems to have swallowed a cup of electricity for breakfast. She's jittery, pacing, talking too fast.

Rafe, in spite of his shaggy, disorganized appearance, is a model of calm, speaking slowly, soothingly. "Tia, Tia, settle down. I can't work with somebody who's as wired as you are. No matter what happens, we're not going to uncover the *Cádiz* today. Most likely, it'll be a long, tedious search that will make you wonder why you ever wanted to come along." He takes a couple of items from his pocket and turns them over in his hand.

"What are those?" she asks. "What are you doing?"

I look at her and wonder where she was the night before. Did Tom, the Quick-Mart guy, call her? Was she with him?

"Okay with you, Nathan, if I put these on your boat?" Rafe asks, holding out his flat hand to show Nathan what's in it.

"What you got there?" Nathan asks.

"My good-luck charms, I suppose you'd call them."
He holds up a bronze medallion about three inches
across and a small bottle full of a yellowish liquid. "The
medallion is a duplicate of one that belonged to the
Duke of Albemarle. He was the patron of Captain William
Phips, who salvaged the *Nuestra Señora de Concepción*
in 1687. He brought up more than twenty-five
tons of silver, and that was considered to be just a fraction
of what there was."

"What does it say?" Tia asks, squinting at the
inscription.

"It says 'Ex Aqua Omnia.' 'Everything comes from the
water.' Nothing is more true than that. Even we, in the
beginning, came from the water."

"Ex Aqua Omnia," she repeats. "What's in the
bottle?"

"That's shark oil. Captain Echeverez, who commanded
the *Nuestra Señora del Carmen* when it sank
in a hurricane in 1715, kept some in his cabin as a
weather indicator. When the oil gets cloudy, bad
weather is on the way."

"Does it really work?" Tia asks. "If it does, Captain
Echeverez should have paid better attention."

"I hope we don't get to find out," Rafe says.

"Sure, put them where you want them," Nathan says.
"I like to know what a man steers himself by. The sea
and the sky are okay with me."

We watch Rafe put a bit of adhesive on the bottom of
the vial of shark oil and on the back of the medallion
and stick them both onto the wood beneath the front
window of the wheelhouse.

"Well, are you ready to find a sunken ship?" he asks.

"Sounds like a good idea," Nathan says. "Brian, you go out there and cast off our line."

We head out from the dock, aiming toward the reef on the other side of Hawk Channel. Rafe believes the *Cádiz* opened her bottom on the reef and sank just inside it. In an effort to save money, and as an indication of his confidence about where the *Cádiz* lies, he has leased only three pinpoint areas. Some parcels around Rafe's are leased to other treasure hunters, and I don't need anybody to tell me what it would feel like to find out that he has miscalculated by a quarter-mile and to have the *Cádiz* found in someone else's lease site.

"What are we going to do today?" I ask.

"Today we tow the magnetometer over our sites on the grid Nathan and I marked yesterday," Rafe says, "recording any hits we get. If we find a cluster of them, we'll go down and have a look. But we're mapping all the lease sites before we get in the water."

"How long will that take?" Tia asks.

"Could take four or five days."

"Four or five *days*?" she says.

"That's just for the mapping. Remember, we could look all summer and not find anything. If treasures were so easy to find, everybody'd be doing it."

She takes herself off to the stern, where she sits watching the boat's wake.

Rafe consults a chart showing the location of his first leased site, and Nathan watches the compass and adjusts the helm. I see Leo alone in the *Crazy Conch* coming along behind us.

TWELVE

When we get to the lease site, Nathan and Rafe consult and talk to Leo on the radio determining the best way to make the sweeps with the magnetometer. We begin the slow trawl along the Styrofoam floats marking the grid lines.

Tia watches the magnetometer screen for a while, waiting for a hit to register. When none does, she begins pacing again, up and down the length of the boat.

"Waiting is the hardest thing in the world," she says as she goes past me.

"You should have brought one of your many books," I say.

"I did," she says. "But I can't concentrate. I want to know for sure that ship's down there."

"You know Mel Fisher searched for sixteen years before he found the *Atocha*, don't you?" Nathan says. "He spent a lot of time hunting in completely wrong places. We could do that, too. Finding treasure needs a long patience."

"But Rafe only has enough funding for this one summer," Tia says. "We have to find it now."

For somebody who a few days ago didn't even want to be involved, she's suddenly gotten very interested in this hunt.

"If we're meant to, we will," Nathan says. "If not . . ." He lets the words hang in the air.

All morning we drag the magnetometer, recording an occasional hit that could be from the *Cádiz* or from a ship a century older or from discarded modern trash.

Tia and I are sent into the galley to make sandwiches for lunch. And, I suspect, to give Tia something to do. Her pacing is making us all nervous.

She slaps mustard on bread slices. "Don't you admire Rafe?" she asks.

"I guess," I say, slicing tomatoes. "Sure. Why not?"

"I mean, look at the risk he's taking, and all this money he's spending. Think of the courage that takes, the sheer nerve."

"I guess," I say again. "But remember, this is a shoestring operation and a lot of people think he's a nut. Besides, he needs to be introduced to a fashion consultant."

She gives me a scornful look. "He has more important things on his mind."

She stands, holding a head of lettuce for so long that I look up from my tomatoes. "What?" I ask.

"Nothing," she says, blinking. "I was just wondering."

"Wondering what?"

"Wondering what it would feel like to be him."

"Him? Why would you want to be him, a mere man?"

"Oh, not *him* necessarily. I mean anybody who's doing what he's doing."

"You're that interested in finding sunken ships?"

She looks at me almost contemptuously. "No. I wish I was."

"Sorry. I don't get it."

"I know." She puts the head of lettuce on the counter and sits down at the wedge-shaped table by the porthole, where she puts her chin in her hand and stares out at the glaze of sun on the water.

I, the guy who's supposed to be so good at figuring things out, have no clue what's going on.

On deck, Rafe munches cheerfully on the sandwiches I ended up making by myself. "It's way too soon to be discouraged, Tia. Don't worry, the *Cádiz*'s down there."

"But I want to know now," Tia says, her eyes invisible behind her dark glasses. "I don't think delayed gratification is a good idea."

Rafe laughs, and a couple of times during the rest of the afternoon he says, "Delayed gratification's not a good idea," and laughs again.

Because the summer days stay light so late, we keep searching until almost eight o'clock, but with no results.

The next day, we do it again. I ride out in the *Crazy Conch* with Leo, wishing I was on the *Angelfish* with Nathan. Once out in the channel, Leo anchors the *Conch* and we board the *Angelfish*. I ignore Tia, which doesn't seem to bother her in the slightest, and sit in the shade reading *Red Sky at Morning*, which is making me laugh out loud, wrenching myself back from New Mexican mountains to Florida waters every time I look up from the page. She doesn't even notice what I'm reading.

The third and fourth days pass the same way, except we leave the *Conch* in Fortunata and all go on the *Angelfish*. Even on a crowded boat, Leo manages to have almost no contact with me. Once he asks me if I'm getting sunburned and a couple of times says something about the weather. The rest of the time he leans on the side studying the water or he's in the wheelhouse or he's glued to the magnetometer screen. Sometimes I feel that he's watching me, but I can't catch him at it. Tia ignores us all, sitting moodily in the stern, gazing at the water, as remote as if she's taken a vow of silence.

While we troll, Rafe gives me instructions in underwater photography of the kind specific to archaeology. I absorb it like a bath sponge.

With the Hasselblad the Guy gave me, I take a lot of pictures of us all, and the boats, and the equipment. There's a boat in the distance, a fishing boat, that I photograph, too.

That night, as we come into Fortunata, I suggest to Tia that she stay ashore the next day. "You're so moody you're making us all nervous." She just raises one eyebrow at me, gives me a sardonic smile, and goes over the side of the *Angelfish* onto the dock.

THIRTEEN

After lunch on the fifth day, as we're finishing our sweep, the magnetometer records a series of hits clustered in the same area.

"This looks interesting," Rafe says. "I think it's time to go down and take a look." For all his calm appearance, he's as anxious as the rest of us to get in the water. "Anybody want to come along?" He gives Tia an amused look.

Without a word, Tia bounces to her feet and begins gathering her scuba stuff.

"Why don't you come, too?" Rafe says to me. "We've all been dry too long. And you need to try out that camera in the actual H2O."

"Great," I say, apprehensive and excited at the same time.

"Now, Miss Tia," Nathan says, "you make sure you

go through all the pre-dive checks. I know you're in a hurry, but you can't be in such a rush that you endanger yourself. You hear?"

"Do I ever forget my pre-dive checks?" she asks, and does them.

Leo volunteers to handle the boat while the rest of us go in. I'm glad. I don't want him watching me underwater while I'm still learning.

It's sunny and clear inside the water, and the sand is like powdered crystal. I can see a long way. The reef is near enough so that there are many more fish here than directly off the dock at Fortunata, and I'm distracted by them, wanting to swim after them, follow them to the reef and see what's there, photograph it and them. They're curious about us, swimming between us almost like pets.

Rafe gives each of us a Ping-Pong paddle just before we dive and this is what we use to fan the sand aside, searching for what has caused the magnetometer hits. We divide the section we're searching into quarters and begin working, with forty minutes' worth of air in our tanks.

I'm clumsy at first, stirring up so much sand that I cloud my own vision and make myself useless. I can see the ease with which Nathan and Rafe work, the grace with which Tia does, and I feel like a hopeless clod. I'm afraid Rafe will be sorry he's ever taken me on.

But gradually, the more I do it and the harder I try, I get the hang of it.

As I'm fanning slowly along, finding nothing but fine, white sand, I feel a tap on my shoulder. Nathan is holding something out to me that looks like a clump of rock. But out of its end sticks the corroded head of an iron nail.

Around his regulator, Nathan is grinning widely.

I raise my eyebrows in question.

Nathan shrugs and nods hopefully. Behind him I can see Rafe holding up something, too. I can't see what it is, but he looks pleased. I take a picture of Nathan and his rock, and some long shots of Tia and Rafe working.

With renewed dedication, I go back to sifting sand. The *Cádiz* could be buried twenty feet under me, I know that. But it could be closer. And maybe the others have found a clue.

But there is nothing in my hole except sand and more sand and water and an occasional chunk of rock. I'm wrenched by disappointment. I guess I don't believe in delayed gratification either. I want to be the one to find the *Cádiz* and I want to find it now.

I keep a nervous eye on my gauges, watching my air and the time. Breathing underwater might seem easy now, but only as long as there's air in my tank.

I've been under, fanning sand around, for thirty-five minutes when Nathan comes up to me and makes the signal for ascent.

I surface and hang on to the diving ladder with the others while we help one another out of our gear and hand it up to Leo.

"I can't believe we were down so long," I say. "It went so fast."

"You got to be careful about that," Nathan says, shaking water off himself like a big brown dog. "Especially when you're working deep. You got to watch your gauges all the time. At one hundred feet you start getting nitrogen narcosis and then you really got to watch yourself. It's like being drunk—you think you can do anything. Many a good diver's gotten in trouble that way. Gary Borders, as experienced as they come, got euphoric at a hundred and seventy feet, threw off his tank, and swam on down. It was his day off, too. He was diving for fun. So you watch it, Brian, you hear me?''

"Right, right," I say, knowing that, one, I'll never be anywhere near one hundred and seventy feet deep, and two, I'll never forget I can't breathe without air.

Rafe spreads out on the deck the handful of items we've brought up. There's Nathan's nail, a couple of iron straps encrusted with coral, a pillow-sized rounded stone, and a thick, round piece of glass that looks like the bottom of a bottle.

"Pretty good," Rafe says. "Promising." He puts his hand on the stone. "This could be a ballast stone. The holds were filled with them to keep those tall, top-heavy ships from tipping over. It didn't always work, but it was a good idea. Of course, it could be just a rock. Be looking for piles of these in the same place. When bottoms tore out, the ballast stones dumped fast." He points at the iron straps. "They could be old enough. And they might be younger. I just don't know yet. The nail . . ." He frowns. "We'll need to find a lot more of them to prove they're from a ship." He turns the round piece of glass. "Could be the bottom of a Coke bottle. But I don't think so. I'm saying it's the bottom of a seventeenth-century brandy bottle. Hey, don't look so disappointed, Brian. What did you think, that we'd go down and there it'd be, just waiting for us?"

Actually, that's exactly what I'd hoped.

Rafe goes on. "Well, that would have been nice, but this stuff is encouraging, really. *Something's* down there, shedding items. If it's not the *Cádiz*, well, then, we'll have found something else."

"Huh," Tia says, exasperated.

"Okay, here's what we do now. We'll go down once more and lay out our grids"—he points to a pile of white piping that can be fitted together to make one-foot-square sections—"so we can know just where each artifact we find comes from. And we'll set up the shooting stand for the camera so all the photos of the search site can be taken from the same elevation and angle. Brian, I want you to get in the habit of bracketing each shot with one stop over and one stop under what the exposure meter indicates. And tomorrow we'll start sifting through our squares one by one."

And that's what we do. For days, using a surface air compressor so we don't have to bother with tanks while we dive, we go through the squares. We bring up tantalizing bits of iron and glass and, once, a bone. That gives me a spooky feeling.

"It's probably from the hold," Rafe says, "not a human bone. The Spanish were notorious for having the filthiest ships afloat. They threw all their trash into the holds, so when the bottoms ripped open, all the trash fell out. Chicken bones, broken crockery, glass. I'm betting that's what a lot of what we're finding is—trash to them, but treasure to us."

But it's not enough treasure for Tia. She's edgy and impatient and goes in at the end of each day cranky and let-down. When I try to soothe or encourage her, she turns her back on me.

"Stop with the Pollyanna stuff," she tells me. "Nothing counts—not nails or broken glass or barrel hoops or spikes, and not all that tedious mapping and recording either. The only thing that counts is the *Cádiz*, and we can't find it." Her voice has tears of frustration in it.

"We will," I say, sticking to Rafe's party line. But even if we don't, I'm finding a different kind of treasure with the photographs I'm taking of the work we're doing, all of it so exotic to me. The underwater color and light are completely new and I can hardly take enough pictures. Rafe loves that he's getting such a complete record of the search. And I love the experience I'm gaining, developing the shots every night with him in Lisbon's bathroom darkroom—including color transparencies he's taught me how to do. And the occasional black-and-white photo that looks more like art than business keeps me going.

"Oh, what does it matter to you?" Tia says. "This is just some vacation gig for you, just some story to tell back in Chicago."

"No," I say. And it's not. The search for the *Cádiz* is changing me in a way I don't yet understand, but I know it's not just some vacation event. It's a trip to a new place that's putting a mark on me.

She stalks away from me.

Nathan's attempts to solace her meet with the same response as mine. Only Rafe can really quiet her. He's so confident, so calm and reassuring. Maybe he doesn't really feel that way, maybe he has as many doubts as the rest of us, but he's able to convince Tia. He stands beside her, murmuring to her, telling her he needs her to keep the faith, praising her diving abilities, and finally she sighs and gives him just enough of a smile to activate her dimple and then we go through the whole routine again the next day.

When we've searched all the squares, we dismantle the grid and move it to the next section of ocean bottom. On the second day in the new location, Rafe finds a pile of stones buried in the sand. We all help clear the sand, and the stones extend through seven squares on the grid.

When we come up at the end of the day, Rafe is elated. "We're getting close. I can smell it. Those are ballast stones, no doubt about it. And where there are ballast stones, there's a ship."

The day after we've found the ballast stones, we find nothing but a few more stones.

We've started the day with such high hopes, such a feeling that we're close, and we finish tired and disappointed.

Hesitantly, Tia says, "Is this anything?" and holds out a hunk of rock.

Rafe takes the rock. With a penknife he pokes around in it, chipping off pieces until he uncovers an edge of something that has to be man-made. He chips some more.

"Well, Tia," he says with a big grin, "this looks to me like a *real de á ocho*, and if it is, we could be in business."

"What's a *real de á ocho*?" she asks.

"It's a piece of eight. A silver coin weighing one ounce minted in the Spanish colonies—Mexico City or Bogotá or Lima. Silver corrodes in salt water, like iron —it gets calcified growths on it"—he taps the rock with the point of his knife—"or it can get eaten away entirely. Not like gold or bronze. They'll be as shiny after three hundred and fifty years underwater as the day they sank."

Tia isn't listening. "A piece of eight? You mean like pirates' pieces of eight, real treasure?" Tia's on her feet now. "You mean we've found it?"

"One *real de á ocho* doesn't mean much," he says. "Not yet. They wash up on the beach after storms if a wreck is anywhere in the neighborhood. A shrimper in Louisiana snagged a wooden chest in his nets in 1973 that contained three hundred pounds of Spanish silver coins dated 1779 to 1783. Nobody knew where it came from, and they still don't. So we've got to find a lot more *reales* and other things, too, before we know we're there."

"I have some more," she says, handing him more rocks.

Once again Rafe chips away with his penknife. "All *right*," he says. "More pieces of eight. Look." He holds the clump out. "There's six or seven coins concreted in here. And I'll guess that these other rocks are the same. We're definitely in the neighborhood."

Then we put the *reales de á ocho* into a sodium hydroxide bath to keep them from drying out before they can be preserved, and go in. This is one trip on which Tia needs no consoling.

FOURTEEN

I hardly sleep that night. And when I do, I dream underwater dreams: aqueous light fanned around me, cartoon treasure chests spilling over with ropes of pearls, golden goblets, flashing rubies, with curious big-eyed fish swimming by.

In the morning I'm light-headed with sleeplessness and excitement.

I fix myself peanut butter toast while Leo drinks coffee and smokes.

"You want some toast?" I ask him.

"Yeah, okay, that'd be good," Leo says. "Say, you're doing all right down there."

"Thanks." I drop bread in the toaster.

"Maybe you and I'll be diving together today."

"Maybe."

"You think we'll find it?"

I'm about to say, "How do I know?" when it occurs to me that Leo might be trying to make conversation with me, an event so rare I don't recognize it at first. "I hope so. I'd like to be in on something like that."

"Yeah," he says. "Me too."

I hand him the plate of toast. "Thanks," he says.

"No problem." I wait, but he doesn't say anything else. "I'm going to get dressed," I say.

So much for conversation between the two of us.

"I'll meet you at the dock," I say on my way through the kitchen again, where Leo's still drinking coffee. I don't need to go so early, but I want out of there.

"There's no hurry," Leo says, looking at his watch.

"I'll help Nathan and Rafe do something," I say, though I think it's probably too early for them, too.

Leo shrugs. "Whatever. I'll be along in a while."

They are there, though, Nathan and Rafe, going over lists, checking out the surface air supply compressor.

"Hi, Brian," Rafe says. "Help me with this checklist, okay? Since I don't have another compressor, we have to make sure we've got what we need to repair this one. If it goes out, we're slowed way down. Spark plugs, fuel line fittings . . ."

We're still counting items on the list when Tia arrives, lugging a picnic basket.

"Mama packed this for the celebration today," she says.

"What celebration?" I ask.

"For when we find the *Cádiz*."

"I doubt we'll be finding it today," Rafe says.

"Mama thinks we will. And if we don't, we'll have a good lunch for consolation." She stands looking at Rafe for a minute with those big golden eyes of hers before she carries the basket into the galley.

That day we eat the lunch for consolation. We spend almost all day in the water and find more tantalizing *reales*, more nails, and a broken piece of chain, but nothing big. All day, while I'm shooting, I think what I'm really photographing is hope.

I take a lot of pictures of Tia. She's graceful enough on land, but underwater she really does seem part fish, with an almost boneless pliancy. And every move she makes seemed worthy of a photograph. I take one of her face-to-face with four little damselfish bumping their noses on her face mask while her hair spreads up and out around her like fan coral. And another of her in a slow-motion leap off the sandy bottom with an encrusted spoon in her hand, the purest expression of joy and discovery that I can imagine. I can hardly take my eyes off her even though she's paying next to no attention to me.

Leo and I work together for a while, and it reminds me of the time I went snorkeling with Tia: underwater he's different. Or maybe it's just that his silence is normal there, not uneasy the way it is on land. Underwater, he pays close attention to me, handing me tools before I need them, watching me work, and yet I don't feel his attention is critical. He just seems interested—maybe more in the project than in me. When we come up I want to say something to him, but I'm not sure what— thank him for his help? For his interest? Anything I can think of seems wrong, so I say nothing.

We work with an air lift, a gadget that sucks sand off

the bottom and deposits it somewhere else at the end of a long tube, effectively digging good holes in the bottom. There's a screen over the end of the tube to keep anything important from being sucked in.

In the next few days we dig a lot of holes and move a lot of sand around, but find nothing except the small, random artifact. Not even any more *reales de á ocho*. All of us are getting pretty frustrated. Rafe worries about hurricanes, since the season begins in July, and Tia is almost crazy again with tension. When nothing more turns up in her sand holes, she almost explodes with bottled need. I have to admit all my nerves feel as if they're about to twang, too, and watching her doesn't make them feel any better.

We spend long midday breaks on the decks of the *Angelfish* and the *Crazy Conch* talking strategy and dreams while we eat the elaborate lunches that Lisbon gets into the habit of making us. Lobster salad sandwiches and bunches of sugared grapes, thermoses of corn chowder and sandwiches of butter and thin slices of cucumber, chicken fried in beer batter and slabs of cornbread made with honey. Every lunch heralds a discovery and is eaten as a consolation.

Yet, in spite of all the talking and the working noise of compressor and air lift, I know one of the things I'll remember most about these days is silence. The silence of the world beneath the surface where surprises can come without the warning of sound and I'm alone with my own breathing and my own yearning.

FIFTEEN

A few days later, close to quitting time, I'm taking a turn with the air lift while Tia and Nathan rest on the *Angelfish*, Leo tends the air compressor, and Rafe prospects with the magnetometer for a better place to dig. I've done this so often with such small results that I'm not paying the attention I should be until I hear the clink of something metal being sucked against the grille of the air lift. I raise the intake hose so it won't draw anything more into it until I can see what has hit the grille.

It's a gold coin, as shiny as the day it was struck.

I wish I could have a picture of what my face looks like right now.

I hold the coin in one hand while I guide the air lift closer to the sand again. As the layers of sand siphon off, I see something I at first don't believe. I blink my eyes and shake my head, but it's still there, a spill of gold coins that extends for several feet in all directions with the splintered remains of a wooden chest at the center of it.

Frantically, I yank at the line that signals Leo to turn off the air lift. I drop it and fall onto my knees, brushing the sand from the coins, crawling through them to see how far the cache extends. I can see Rafe in the distance poking around in the sand, but there's no way I can call to him, and I'm afraid to leave what I've found for fear that it will disappear before I can get back to it.

I realize I'm breathing too fast, gulping air and hyperventilating. I slow my breaths. Then I remember the camera. Pictures first, before I do anything else.

I take my time, forcing myself to be careful, thorough, precise, planting markers, making sure the shooting stand is steady, doing it the way Rafe wants it, the way it has to be. I make my shots, taking more than I strictly need.

Then I'm free to go nuts.

I scoop some of the coins into the collecting bucket, dropping and spilling them in my haste, and then, finding the bucket too heavy to lift, I pour some out again. I grab the bucket and kick frantically over to Rafe. He turns to me, his eyebrows lifted in surprise. I shove the bucket under his nose and grab his arm, pointing to where I've been working. I don't have to do anything more to convince him to follow me.

When he sees the pile of shining gold coins against the sand, he pounds me on the back in the slow-motion way that water allows and we hold on to each other and jump languidly up and down, our flippers clashing. It's like being mimes.

He gestures to the surface, and though I'm afraid to leave what we've found, I follow him to the boat.

He breaks the water screaming. "We're there! We're there!" Water streams from his beard and he shakes his head, scattering drops that fly out like circus spangles.

Nathan is at the ladder. "Pipe down," he says.

"Why should we?" Rafe asks. "I think we've hit pay dirt. Wait'll you see—"

"Somebody's watching us," he says.

Rafe stops, his mouth open. "Watching? What do you mean?"

"Out there," Nathan says. "There's a boat. The *Pelican*. That's how close it is, I can read the name through the binoculars. They're not on any of our sites, but they're right at the edge. And their glasses are on us."

"That boat's been there every day," I say. "I took some shots of it."

Rafe becomes serious. His eyes are narrow. "Okay," he says. "We're going to have to be very, very careful." He turns to me. "Brian, have you got a telephoto lens on your camera?" I nod. "I want you to take a lot more pictures of the *Pelican* and her crew. And don't worry about them seeing you." He's pulling himself up the ladder, passing my specimen bucket quickly to Nathan, whose eyes widen when he sees what's in it, and then quickly his face is neutral again.

Nathan and Rafe go below with the bucket. Leo and Tia join them. I stay topside, fitting the telephoto lens to the Hasselblad. My big moment, stolen from me as surely as if the *Pelican* had stolen my bucket of doubloons or whatever they are. Now I won't be there to see Leo's reaction to my being the one to find the gold, to see him forced to recognize my value to this operation. Without me there, he doesn't have to pretend to be proud of me. Or maybe he wouldn't bother to pretend. And maybe it's just as well I'm not there to see that.

I make sure the telephoto lens is on tight.

I focus on the *Pelican*. There are two guys in shorts and baseball caps facing me, looking close enough to punch. All they're doing is leaning on the *Pelican*'s rail and watching, but their anchor is out and they aren't fishing. I remember PeeWee's mentioning some other guys looking for treasure near Fortunata. Maybe the treasure they're looking for is the one we're about to find.

I shiver. How easy it would be for them to come over tonight after we're gone, to come underwater on Hydro-Scooters with big headlights and take everything we've found. I shake my head and keep shooting. They're probably vacationers from Cleveland anchored to admire the scenery and I'm a paranoid nut case. But Nathan thinks they're suspicious. So maybe he's paranoid, too. It's easy to get that way when you've stumbled onto a pile of gold coins.

The guys in baseball caps weigh their anchor while I shoot, and begin motoring slowly back toward the Keys. Probably going back to the motel to tell their wives about the strange kid on the *Angelfish* who took their pictures this afternoon.

Rafe comes up the companionway from below and looks at the departing *Pelican*.

"Sightseers?" I say.

"Hmmm," he says, and I'm glad not to feel so paranoid anymore.

Then he claps me on the shoulder so hard my knees almost buckle. "Good job, Brian," he yells. He grabs my other shoulder and shakes me. "Fantastic job! Am I glad you came to Mosquito Key. Not just a gifted photographer, but a nascent archaeologist with the kind of nose for where to look that's worth all the gold in that bucket."

"Is it really gold?" I ask, trying to stay casual with these compliments. I don't deserve the one about the golden nose—finding the coins was a pure accident—but I am a good photographer. It feels right and I know it.

"Yes, Brian, it's really gold. Now all we have to do is find an ingot with a name on it that matches a name on the passenger list, and we've got our proof it's the *Nueva Cádiz*. Then I'll be able to get all the investors I want. We'll have fancy equipment coming out our ears and we'll put this baby in the history books."

"What do you mean, with a name on it?"

"Gold ingots—silver ones, as well—always belonged to someone: the King of Spain or a private party. To prevent any—ah—unfortunate misunderstandings, the owners had their names, usually the date, and sometimes the name of the vessel they were traveling on etched into the bar. The name of the vessel's not so important if the name of the owner is on the passenger list. Passengers smuggled a lot of stuff that wasn't on the manifest for the same reasons they do now, to avoid paying taxes and duties. But they still put their names on their things. And not just on their gold and silver but on their razors, belt buckles, cups, and plates, too. It wasn't so easy then to pop down to the mall and replace what you'd lost, so they wanted to make sure no one else could steal something and pass it off as his own. Same idea as etching your social security number onto your computer or CD player, so the cops can recover it if it's stolen."

"But no names on coins?"

"Nope. But the dates on them are right—1640s. Don't worry," he adds. "This is it. I'm sure of it. It's just a question of time before we find the proof. Now let's keep our fingers crossed that everything'll be in our lease sites and no hurricanes come along to mess things up."

Tia, Nathan, and Leo have come on deck as Rafe is speaking, and except for Tia, who has an eerie kind of calm, they seem as excited as he and I are.

I risk sounding like a paranoid nut case in front of them all. "Do you think we should leave one of the boats out here tonight? Just in case the *Pelican* comes back?"

Nobody laughs, but Leo gives me an odd look that I interpret to mean he thinks I'm being an alarmist. Tia doesn't seem to be paying attention, but Rafe says to Nathan, "What do you think?"

"I don't know," Nathan says. "Maybe we overreacted. How about we keep an eye out, see if they turn up again. Could have just been curious fishermen."

I'm astonished when Leo says, "If it'll make you feel better I can come back out in the *Conch* and spend the night. But it'll be well after dark before I can get my stuff together and get back out here."

Rafe thinks for a minute. "Okay," he says. "It would

make me feel better. Let's wrap it up for today, then. I want to get this gold into the vault in Marathon. And I'll develop today's photos, Brian. You get a night off.''

The bank manager in Marathon has agreed to open the vault at any hour to store whatever valuables Rafe finds. One of the advantages of living in the Keys, I guess. I try to imagine getting a Chicago banker to open the vault by himself at 9 p.m. for somebody who looks like Rafe.

SIXTEEN

In the gathering twilight, we ride back on the *Angelfish*. I know my mind is full of treasure and I'll bet Rafe's and Nathan's are, too. As for Tia and Leo, who could even guess what goes on in there.

As soon as we dock, Tia hops over the side and sets off down the dock barefoot, swinging her sandals in her hand. Each dock lamp lights her shape for an instant as she passes it, and then she fades into a shadow again, as if she's briefly coming back to a brighter self before sinking again into her troubled and troubling silence.

I look after her and back to Nathan, who's buttoning things up on board. He jerks his head toward her and gives me a gesture, indicating I should go after her. I just stand looking at him, uncertain. He frowns and jerks his head again and this time I go, but I don't know why.

She must hear me running after her, but she doesn't turn.

"Tia!" I call, but she doesn't stop.

I catch up with her and take her by the arm, which she jerks out of my grasp, but at least she stops.

"What's going on?" I ask her.

She looks me in the face for the first time in days, and I almost flinch from the expression in her eyes.

"What do you care?" she asks fiercely.

I open my mouth and close it and open it again, but I can't think of what to say.

She whips away and starts walking again, and I come back to life. "Hey!" Who does she think she is, dismissing me like I'm some peasant and she's the Queen? Is this what she's been thinking about through all her silent, brooding hours? How to be rude to me? "What is your problem? You think you're so good you don't even have to answer me? You think you get to make your own rules? Ones that say it's okay to treat me like dirt?"

I keep up with her, leaning into her face, and I'm way angrier with her than I should be. Where is all this anger coming from?

By now we're off the dock, standing in the road. She seems undecided which way to go, and while she hesitates, I take her arm again and pull her off the road and down onto the scruffy little gravel beach. She struggles but not hard enough so I believe it.

"Sit down," I say and shove her onto the coarse sand. Never in my life have I exerted any strength against a female person. I've never been in a real fistfight, and the last shoving match I participated in was in the sixth grade, though I haven't forgotten how close I came to hitting Leo that night in the kitchen. I have to admit, there is a weird thrill in pushing someone around, a scary kind of power trip. Especially somebody like Tia, who's ordinarily so hard to push. I'm going to have to watch this.

When she plops down, there's still enough light for me to see the surprised look on her face.

I sit down next to her. "Tia," I say in my gentlest voice, penance for my roughness, "talk to me." I repeat what Nathan said to me the morning after Rafe hired me that made such an impression. "I can listen."

She bolts up and runs away from me, straight into the water. I watch while she swims out, with strong strokes, maybe a hundred feet. Then she turns on her back and lies there, her arms out at her sides.

I'm already barefoot, but I pull off my T-shirt, ready to go after her if I have to.

She floats for a long time, until I have a headache from trying to see her as it becomes completely dark. It seems to me that she could disappear in an instant if I take my eyes off her. Finally she turns on her stomach and swims in, her strokes slow and heavy.

She wades onto the beach, her hair and clothes streaming water. Her burnished skin gleams with wetness and I can't tell if the moisture on her face is seawater or tears. She walks toward me, kicks her sandals out of the way, and sits down next to me again.

"Are you okay?" I ask, but she doesn't answer.

"Oh, you wouldn't understand," she finally says in a weary tone of voice. "How could you? Everything's so easy for you. You've never felt all explosive with bottled-up frustration, never felt like a permanent disappointment, never worried you wouldn't—oh, forget it.''

To my great astonishment, she puts her face into her arms crossed on top of her knees, and bursts into tears.

I think about patting her on the back but decide against it. Nothing else comes to my mind, so I just wait.

Finally she slows down, gasping and hiccuping, and turns her face, still resting on her arms, to me. The tears on her face shine in the dark with the same gleam of the dock lamps on the water. She sniffles juicily and I can't help laughing.

"That was gross," I say. "Don't you have a Kleenex?"

She shakes her head and then wipes her nose with the wet sleeve of her T-shirt.

"Lisbon's going to love finding that in the laundry," I say.

She makes a watery sound that might be a laugh.

I don't know where to go from there, so I wait some more.

Finally she speaks. "I hate to admit I even think this, but it's true," she says. "I'm just so jealous of you."

Of all the things I imagined were on her mind, from Tom, the Quick-Mart guy, to communicating with space aliens, to whether she should change her hairdo, that was one thing that hadn't even come close to occurring to me. "Huh?" I say intelligently. "For what?"

"For your—oh, I can't say it. It makes me feel too weak."

"You have to say it now. You can't leave me out here wondering like this."

She takes a deep breath. "For your . . ." She pauses and starts again. "For your skin."

"My skin—" I start to say, and then I get it. I'm white

and she's not. Somehow I'd thought it wouldn't matter down here in the remote Keys, in spite of how much it seemed to be on the minds of Lisbon and Nathan. It hasn't mattered to me. After the first moment I saw Tia, when I noticed her color, I haven't thought about it again; I've just been intrigued with her. It occurs to me that I'm naïve and insensitive, and I'm ashamed.

"I'm sorry," I say. "I can't say I understand because I don't."

"No, you don't," she says, and her eyes glitter with reflected light. "When people look at you they have no ideas about you. They wait for you to show them something. That's not true when they look at me."

"What do they think when they look at you?" I ask.

She moves a shoulder. "Sometimes they wonder if I'm easy. Or if I can read. Or if I'm honest. Or if I'm pregnant. And that's just the beginning. Nathan says he came down here because he's a big ugly black man and he got tired of people on the street either wanting to fight with him or being afraid of him. He just wants to live. So do I."

I can't think of anything to say. I can't imagine her life.

"You've never had somebody come up to you on the street and say, 'You know, I just hate niggers,' have you?"

I shake my head.

"Or had a guy sneak out to see you because he knows his parents would have a fit if they knew he wanted to be with somebody they'd call a nigger."

I wonder if she's talking about Tom. I shake my head again.

"And on top of all that I've got Mama and Nathan

pushing, pushing all the time for me to be everything, like some kind of SuperBlackWoman. To be a shining example and a hero and a success story, perfect in every way." She puts her head back on her knees. "I'm tired."

I don't blame her. "I know I can't understand about being black, but the pushing is something I do understand. My mother's the same way."

"So what do you do about it?"

"Ignore her. Do my own stuff."

She sighs. "Maybe it's easier for guys to ignore their mothers than for girls. And you're lucky again. You know what your own stuff is. I think I'd be better off if I had something I was passionate about, the way you are about photography, but I don't. That's why I envy Rafe, too. He knows what he wants to do and he's doing it full steam, even when it's hard. It seems like I can do everything about equally well and I don't really care about any of it."

"Well, maybe that's how you start," I say, trying to recall why I got going on photography, or computers, or anything else. I can't remember. I tried them, the way lots of other people do, but for some reason I stayed with them. A match of personality to activity in some strange way. "Just do anything. Do it while you wait for something else. You never know when it'll happen. Or maybe one of your time-killers will turn into something more." I feel as if I'm babbling, but I want to help her so much that I'm struggling for an answer. I can't do anything about the color thing, but maybe I can about the other problem. It can't have been easy for her to say the things she has to me, and I want to be equal to her confidence.

"Don't patronize me," she says, all bristly again. "I know what I'm talking about and you don't. Some people just drift all their lives, nothing comes. Look at Leo."

Was that Leo's problem, that he'd never found something he could be passionate about? What about Mom? What about me?

"Or worse," she goes on, "there *is* something you love, but you aren't any good at it."

"That's an easier problem," I say, and I mean it. I can speak with experience now, about the awful, awkwardly composed, poorly lit or focused photographs I took at first, but how they got better the more I worked at them. I tell her all this, and then I say, "I hear you wrote a story."

Her head comes up. "Who told you that?"

"Lisbon." I'm afraid to say more, to have her think I'm insulting or patronizing her, but I go on. "I bet it was good."

She lowers her head again. "I thought so. And please don't tell me I gave up too easy, the way Mama and Nathan do. I'll decide that."

"Okay," I say.

She's leaning forward, drawing in the sand with her finger, though it's too dark for me to see what she's drawing. Maybe she's writing. "You're smart," I say. "And strong. You can get to be good at whatever you choose."

She sighs and moves so she can lean her head on my shoulder. "I don't know. It takes so long. And you know how I am about delayed gratification."

Her voice sounds tired. I remember that feeling from

childhood—of having cried or tantrumed for so long that it's a relief to stop.

"Nathan says looking for hidden treasure is a long patience," I say. "Anyway, what else are you going to do with your time?" Then I hear myself say, "What's so odd is that I've been envying you."

She raises her head. "Me? Whatever for?"

She's been honest with me, so I have to be with her. "For Nathan. Your father."

"He's not my—" She stops. "Well, you're right, of course. He wasn't the sperm donor, but he's the father." She turns her face to mine. Her dark skin blends into the darkness so that she's only a shadow, a shadow with eyes that catch the hidden light and gleam at me. "I thought your mother got married again."

"She did, but not to someone who wants to be my father. He thinks I'm too old to need one."

"Oh," she says and puts her hand on my back. Slowly she strokes from my neck to my waist, and then does it again.

The instant before I'm so distracted by her touch that I can't think, it occurs to me that neither one of us has even bothered to consider defending Leo's fathering abilities.

I reach around and take her hand in mine. "You'd better stop," I say.

She yanks her hand out of mine. "Why? I'm not good enough for a nice white city boy?" She jumps to her feet.

"No, Tia, that's not it at all." I get up, too. I'm embarrassed to tell her that it felt *too* good, and I was afraid of what I might do next, which might have insulted her more. I try to make a joke. "Remember, I'm just a useless male."

Still angry, she says, "You know I didn't mean that. I was just saying that to provoke you, to start something."

"How was I supposed to know *that*? I'd barely met you. And you don't know anything about me if you think I'd think I was too good for you. It seems more the other way around."

"You saying I'm conceited?"

"Not quite. But you aren't exactly a picnic, either. And sometimes I like that, I admit it. But I don't like being attacked."

"I don't have to force guys into wanting to be with me," she says haughtily, looking out to sea with her chin high.

"I didn't say I don't like being with you," I say, "but sometimes it can feel a lot like carrying something heavy up a steep hill; a lot of work."

She continues to stare. "So don't bother," she says.

"We do have to work together. That'll be easier if we can be friendly."

"Well, fine." Her voice is curt. "We'll be friendly."

"Why does everything have to be so hard with you? Or are you just some kind of drama queen, hogging the spotlight?"

She turns to me fast, and for a moment I think she's going to hit me. And her behavior is no more of a surprise to me than my own. Why don't I just leave her alone to stew in her own mercurial juices?

"What difference does it make to you?" she practically spits at me. "You'll be leaving soon. That's one thing men are good at."

I'm about to ask her how many hundreds of men have left her when I remember her father. Maybe all it takes is one. Or maybe there have been others—of Lisbon's or of hers.

"Not all of them," I say. "This is pointless. I need some dinner and some sleep and so do you. It's late and you're soaked. Lisbon'll be wondering where you are. Go home. I'll see you tomorrow."

"Thanks, Mom," she says sarcastically. "I'll go home when I feel like it."

"Okay," I say. "Spend the night here if you want."

I make my way to the road and look back at her dark shape silhouetted against the silver and black of the water. I turn toward Leo's and then I reverse myself and walk down the road to the End of the Rainbow. I lean against the gumbo-limbo tree and wait.

I can see Nathan inside talking to Lisbon, the two of them looking like an illustration of the concept of harmony in some New Age dictionary. She's sitting in a white rocking chair with a high back and flowered cushions. He's balanced on the arm of it—I worry about it breaking under him—looking down at her while she talks, his hand lightly on her cheek. The table lamp powders them with gold, and I envy Tia again, and feel outraged at her rudeness toward them, even though I sense her kind of rudeness comes from feeling loved enough to permit it. Why can't she absorb some of the peace and good humor that surround her and just deal with the rest?

After a while I hear her sandals slapping along the

street. She passes me going up the walk, head down, so she doesn't see me, and stamps up the stairs. I see Lisbon and Nathan turn their heads, anticipation on their faces, as she slams the door.

I head for Leo's, where no one's waiting for me.

SEVENTEEN

The next morning Tia sits in the stern of the *Angelfish* with a notebook in her lap. Her hair is pulled severely back and braided tightly and she never takes off her dark glasses. She writes in the notebook all the way out to the orange marker buoys over our search site.

I take pictures, or pretend to, but mostly I'm looking at her through the viewfinder. How can I be so attracted to her, exasperated by her, sorry for her, and baffled by her all at the same time?

We set out our six-point mooring head on to the prevailing wind and sea, with the head moor the heaviest, and when we're done, there's the *Pelican* approaching from the Keys.

"Hey," I say to Nathan, "are they arming their cannons yet?"

"Not yet," he says, still looking out. "But don't treat

this as a joke. Piracy is alive and well in these waters. Not just over drugs, either. Piracy is about anything of value. The *Cádiz* qualifies."

"You really think they're watching us?"

"Now I know they are."

"Will they know what we find when we find it?"

"Bet on it. Maybe we won't know how they know, but it doesn't matter, does it?"

"You're scaring me."

"Being scared ain't a bad thing. It keeps you alert. It's when your sense of danger gets blunted that you're in the most trouble."

Leo comes over from the *Conch* and tells us that he sat up most of the night but saw nothing. Then he returns to the *Conch* to get some sleep while we start our workday.

I watch the *Pelican* for a while, riding up and down on the waves, so white and calm and patient.

"So what do we do?" I ask Nathan and Rafe.

"Watch them back," Rafe says, "until they try something. Stay alert. That's all. Go on with our work."

Nathan and I begin readying the air compressor and the other equipment, and Rafe does something in the wheelhouse.

"How long have you known Tia?" I ask, making sure she's still in the stern.

"A week longer than I've known Lisbon," he says. "About eight years. She's how I first got to talking to Lisbon. They just moved back to Mosquito Key from Miami, and Lisbon was working on the End of the Rainbow, trying to get it in shape to open up. Tia used to come down to the docks to watch what was going on, and to get out of Lisbon's way. She was bright as new paint, all brushed and braided and ironed to a fare-thee-well. It was plain somebody was taking good care of her. And could she ask questions! Pretty soon I said to her, 'You planning to buy my boat, child, is that why you want to know so much about it?' She said they couldn't afford to buy one more thing until the End of the Rainbow started making them some money, but when it did, she was going to bring me home to meet her mama and then she was going to buy my boat." He stopped to laugh his deep rich laugh that felt like a bath in warm chocolate. "Well, I told her I thought I'd better meet her mama right away if we were going to do business together one day, and how about if I bought them some supper that night. Course, Lisbon was mortified her little firecracker had started all this, but I think Miss Tia was an instrument of destiny. First time I laid eyes on Lisbon I knew she was what I'd been waiting for most of my life. And I'm a lucky man that it turned out to be that way for her, too. So it's no wonder I have a real soft spot for Miss Tia, no matter how much trouble she is, but I'd feel that way about her even if I wasn't just a plain fool for her mother." He stared out to sea for a while. "She tell you what's on her mind last night?"

I nod.

"Think she'll be okay?"

I shrug. "Probably. She's pretty tough. It's going to take a while, though."

"I thank you for your effort," he says formally. "And I apologize for pressing you to go after her. Just seemed to me she needed someone to talk to and that maybe you could get more out of her than I've been able to lately."

"No problem," I say.

"You're on your way to being a good man," he says. "The world needs a load more of them."

I make an embarrassed sound and head for the bow to get a wrench, rolling more than I really have to, giving myself the swagger of a seventeenth-century seaman, imagining the deck under my feet to be that of the *Nueva Cádiz*. No matter how much I swagger, though, I can't really show how proud Nathan's words have made me feel. If he'd seen my actual performance with Tia he might not have said them, but for now I don't care.

I volunteer to man the compressor while the others dive. I had my fun yesterday; today they can count the coins I found. Which, given my paranoia about the *Pelican*, I'm hoping are still where I left them.

Rafe isn't down long before he's up again.

"What?" I ask.

"Those coins," he says. "They aren't where they should be. And the marker's gone." He comes up the ladder fast. "I want to look at those pictures you took yesterday."

"Where are they if they aren't where they should be?" I ask. "Maybe the sand shifted and buried them again." I look over my shoulder, across the water, to the *Pelican*.

He gives me a look. "I thought of that." He doesn't sound annoyed, quite, but I get the idea; of course he'd have thought of that. "They aren't anywhere."

"What? All of them? There were so many."

He's in his files, pulling out the pictures from the day before. "Oh, there's still a few down there, but not what I remember." He spreads the pictures out on the chart table and studies them, muttering and moving his fingers over them, measuring. The plastic grid laid over the search site makes it easy to locate the things we've found in the pictures, so I know he hasn't made a mistake. Finally he nods and looks up. "I think somebody paid us a visit last night. They must have come early, just after dark, before Leo came back in the *Conch*."

"The *Pelican*?" I ask, but it's not really a question.

He looks out across the water at the sleek white boat. Even at this distance we can see the two men in the stern, fishing. "They're the obvious ones, of course. But there's not a shred of evidence."

"So what are we going to do?" I ask.

"Couple of things," he says. "We're going to be very careful how we bring anything up, keep it as quiet as possible. And we're going to leave a boat out here every night with two people keeping watch. They can't dive without lights at night. And with lights, we'll see them."

"And then what?" I ask. "Do we go down to scare them away?" I'm imagining knife fights in dark water, severed air hoses, the drama of old black-and-white movies.

"Are you kidding?" he says. "Who do you think we are, Arnold Schwarzenegger?" He laughs. "We call the Marine Patrol on the radio and get them out here. And we keep very good photos and records of our work so we can tell if anything's been disturbed. Perfect provenance. We're archaeologists, not heroes. Brains are more important than brawn, and they usually last longer."

I laugh, simultaneously relieved and disappointed. I don't really mind the vision of myself doing something heroic. Especially in front of Tia.

EIGHTEEN

The rest of the day goes okay except that Tia never speaks to me. I go down to take photos of what's left of the coins and then we bring them all up. We find more things: broken crockery, a wall of ballast stones, a piece of a pottery shaving mug. Nothing yet that proves this is the *Nueva Cádiz*, but none of us has any doubt.

The *Pelican* stays with us most of the day, finally motoring in about five. That's when Leo goes in, too, in the *Crazy Conch* to pick up some supplies for Nathan and me, since we're going to stay out on the *Angelfish* overnight. Nathan and I each make a careful list for him of what we want. I'm not crazy about his rummaging around in my drawers, but there's no choice.

He comes back, drops off the groceries and our gear, and takes Tia and Rafe and our day's finds away with him.

It's strange to be out on the water this way, with evening coming. The compressor's off, so it's quieter than it's been all day and I can hear the little sounds of waves lapping the sides of the boat. Nathan's sitting in a canvas chair in the stern, his feet up on the rail, sipping a beer, a bowl of pretzels on the deck beside him.

"Hey, Brian, get yourself a drink and come sit with me. We've had ourselves a long day."

I bring a lemonade from the galley and join him.

"Better eat some of these pretzels before the sea air turns them to mush," he says. "I'll fix us a real dinner later."

We sit, watching the sun approach the horizon. It's huge and blood-red and there's something almost frightening about how hot and fierce it looks, and how close. The sight of it silences us and we watch. I'm in awe as it touches the water and regally lowers itself in. As the last fiery edge of it disappears, there's a burst of neon green where sea meets sky, so strong and bright it hurts my eyes. By the time I blink, it's gone.

"Did you see that?" I ask Nathan, not trusting my own vision. I'm standing, leaning forward across the rail.

He nods, slow and satisfied, not wired and semi-freaked the way I am. "The famous green flash. A rare thing, son. You could wait a long time before you see that again." He sips his beer.

I sit again, trying to re-create it in my mind.

"The world is full of strange things," he says. "I saw a few of them when I was in the Navy, traveling around. Fish that fly and climb trees, and men who can stick pins through their tongues. Animals that eat their own children and men who might as well. And then something like that green flash." He sighs. "I don't even want to know why it happens. It's enough for me that it does. I like a lot of mystery—reminds me that man's not everything."

We sit there while the darkness comes, settling softly over us like a cloud. The sun heat of the day is gone and the air is warm and soft—I feel that I could pull it around me like a blanket and sleep.

I'm not even sure when Nathan gets up and heads to the galley.

He fixes pasta with some great kind of sauce, and strawberries with sour cream and brown sugar for dessert. He makes it look easy, not like Leo, who can mess up the whole kitchen boiling a hot dog.

We eat on the deck, watching the water, and when we're finished we sit in our chairs at the stern, our feet up on the railing, having a last cup of spirited Louisiana coffee—Nathan says it has guts. We're contented men.

"You're one great cook," I tell Nathan. "As good as Lisbon."

"Well, people usually get good at what they like to do, and Lisbon and I do like to cook. Makes sense. You won't keep working on what you don't enjoy."

I've just said this to Tia. To hear Nathan say it, confirming my instinct, is intensely satisfying. I seek more confirmation. "Even if you're awful at it?"

"Hardly anybody's born knowing how to do anything. Look how hard learning to walk is. But you want to, so you keep doing it."

"Now," I say, feeling pleased and wise, "if I could just figure out how to be as suave and charming with the ladies as you are. Am I going to need years of practice for that?"

"Oh, son," Nathan says, serious as a preacher, "I don't think you can ever achieve that. I mean, I *am* the standard of suaveness for the world. Sort of the high-water mark of charm."

"Excuse me. I lost my head there for a minute," I say.

"Any particular lady you'd like to charm?" Nathan asks. "Miss Tia, by chance?"

"Oh, man. I'd have to be some Ph.D. in snake-charming to make a dent in her. That is a charm-resistant person."

"Oh, I wouldn't say she's charm-resistant. Just charm-suspicious. It may be that charm's not what she needs."

"Well, let's just say, hypothetically, that I was interested in her—what should I do?"

Nathan drains his coffee cup and wipes his mouth carefully with his napkin. "She's always been sassy as a redbird, and full of ideas to hit you over the head with. But one thing Miss Tia's always hated is anybody feeling sorry for her. Makes her feel inadequate somehow. So that's what not to do." He gives me a sidelong look I can barely see in the faint light from the galley. "You know a friendship has to work both ways. Her kind of sass and vinegar might be just the thing for a boy with a sadness."

I look over at him. The light behind him makes him just a big black shadow next to me, the kind of shadow I'd have been afraid of if I didn't know it was Nathan, who I couldn't have been afraid of in any circumstance that I can think of. But somehow what he says gives me a little thrill in my stomach that I can think is fear if I want to.

"What makes you think I'm sad?" I ask.

"Aren't you?"

I search around in my head. I haven't gone very far before I stumble over what feels like a lot of sadness.

"Well, everybody's sad about something, aren't they?" I say.

"That's probably true. I'm sad about the things I can't change—stuff that happened to me as a kid, stupid choices I made. But I know all that makes me who I am today, and he's a person I like okay, so it tempers the sadness." He's quiet for a while as the waves plash against the boat, simple, lulling sounds. Then he says, "The best thing you can do with Miss Tia is be honest. Tell her the truth. And then you better be careful with her."

"What do you mean? Is she dangerous?"

"You might be dangerous to her. If she gets to trusting you."

"I'm as far from dangerous as you can get."

"Now you listen to me." His big shadow sits up and turns in my direction. "I was a young man once, your age, and I know what those hormones can do to your brain. What they do is turn it off. Mixing black and white is still a touchy thing in a lot of places, so that's hard enough. And I'm thinking that the best thing for the two of you to do is stay on the friendship level. Nobody's got too many friends. And we don't need no unexpected babies around here to mess up a couple of futures."

I sit up, too. "Hey, I would never—" Well, maybe not *never.* After all, Tia is crazily beautiful to me, and my hormones are all in working order, from what I can tell. But I'd need a lot more cooperation from her than I'm likely to get.

"Well, that's all fine," he says. "Because I don't want

anything chancy happening to her. But while we're talking, I'm not just telling you about Miss Tia. I'm telling you about any girl—all those future girls who'll be yours when you take my charm lessons. Don't you go getting mixed up with any woman you'd be embarrassed to bring home to dinner with your mama. And don't you go forgetting that you're half of any pair, with more than half the responsibility for taking care of both of you. You get what I'm saying? I'm talking about birth control and diseases and like that."

"Nathan," I say, and stop. Is this the birds-and-bees conversation that fathers are supposed to have with their sons? If so, here I am, a person with a father *and* a stepfather, getting the talk from a man who is no one's father. At least not one in the biological sense. What else makes a man a father?

"I'm listening," he says. Words I've never heard from Leo.

And then my sadness, my unkept secret from myself, has a name.

"Me too," I say. "I heard you."

He leans back and looks up at the stars. "You know, in this world, it's hard to be a good man. There's a lot of things—the movies, TV, the bad example of famous people who should know better—all pulling at you to cut some corners, make excuses, think just about yourself. And this world needs good men now more than it has in a long time. You think you want to be one of those? It ain't always an easy thing."

I've never thought of myself as anything but good, but the way he's talking, I'm starting to see the road ahead of me as an attractive minefield. What do I need to be armed for it?

"How?" I ask.

"You need you some good men to imitate. You got some?"

"Not enough," I say, wondering if one is enough if he's the right one.

"Work on that. It's the most important thing you'll do."

I feel the pushing from Nathan that Tia complains about, but somehow, right now, I don't mind.

The silence stretches out before us like a contented animal in a sunny spot.

"Nathan?"

"Yeah?"

"Why aren't you and Lisbon married?" It's the kind of question I've never asked anybody; a question that feels intrusive and offensive. But I can ask Nathan because he will tell me the truth. Besides, I need to know why Nathan, a good man, isn't doing the right thing for his woman.

His sigh is heavy. "It's her, not me. She was married once, to Tia's father, and she's afraid. She thinks marriage'll change what we have, make it ordinary. I keep working on her, though, trying to convince her it'll be more extraordinary."

"Is that why you're the way you are with Tia?"

"I'm that way because I love her mother, so it's my duty and my pleasure to be a father to Miss Tia whether she likes it or not. That girl needs my love and my help."

There is silence again.

"Nathan?"

"Yeah?"

"What *is* a father?"

He's quiet for a while and I hear him breathe deeply before he speaks. "Well, I didn't have one, so I'm flying by the seat of my pants, making it up as I go along. But I think it's somebody who puts your welfare in the front of his mind, who'll make himself available to you for any question, any problem, any heaviness that falls upon you. Forever. At least, that's what I wanted for myself. And still want. You never outgrow that, I don't think."

Oh, Leo, I think, and wonder what my grandfather was like, where Leo took his own fathering lessons. Fatherless, childless Nathan seems to understand more than Leo, who had a father and is one, whose own father was around until he was a married man.

Nathan claps his hands onto his knees and stands up. "You get to do the dishes, Brian, while I set up the checkerboard. Maybe you've noticed the *Pelican*'s back out there."

I hadn't. I'd been too intent on what Nathan was telling me. But now that I see the *Pelican*'s lights bobbing in the night, I get a dark rush of anxiety and foreboding. I hurry to the well-lit galley and the commonplace reassurance of soapy dishwater.

NINETEEN

Later, with one eye on the *Pelican* and the other on the checkerboard, I'm surprised that I can still feel so tired. When I've yawned for about the tenth time, Nathan says, "You better sleep first while I keep watch. I'll wake you in four hours."

I nod and stumble off to bed, falling into it still in my shorts and T-shirt.

It seems like a minute later, not four hours, that Nathan is shaking my shoulder. "Your turn," he says. "It's three o'clock." I struggle up from a thick, blank sleep.

"Anything happening?" I ask, trying to clear my head, muddled with sleep.

He shrugs. "Nothing I can see, but the *Pelican*'s still out there with running lights and one light on below-decks." He flops back into the other bunk. "Wake me at six-thirty."

On deck, the air is still and warm and I feel very small in the big night. The moon is low, but making enough light for me to see the outline of the *Pelican*. They must know we're suspicious or we wouldn't be spending the night out here. Are they stupid enough to try something under our very noses? Or do they think they've waited long enough for us to give up and go to bed?

Keeping watch when nothing is happening is unbelievably boring. I sit, I stand, I get something to drink, I wander. I look at my watch. It's 3:37. This will be a long night.

I sit in my chair in my favorite position, feet on the rail, drinking lemonade, and watching the moonlight shimmer on the water. It takes me too long to suspect that the light I'm watching isn't *on* the water but *under* it. I sit up and stare, watching the light move. Now that I'm paying attention I think I can tell that it's actually two lights.

I'm paralyzed. Whatever hero delusions I might have had evaporate in an instant. I have absolutely no idea what to do. I stand up. I should wake Nathan, who by now has been asleep for less than forty-five minutes.

I go below and stand in the doorway. He's on his back, one arm flung over his eyes, snoring like a freight train.

I can't make myself wake him for what could turn out to be nothing. I'm still not sure if it's a trick of the moonlight or some kind of tropical-waters phosphorescent phenomenon.

I go back topside and look for the lights. They're still there, about ten yards off the port side, where we were working this afternoon, and they're stationary now. Somehow I can't really believe it's the guys from the *Pelican*, that they would be bold enough to raid our site while we're right on top of it. Or I don't want to believe it. I'm also afraid of looking like a fool if I wake Nathan and call the Marine Patrol out at 4 a.m. for a hallucination. I grab the Nikonos V, the exposure meter, and a length of rope, clap a mask and snorkel on my head, and go over the side and down the diving ladder. With the camera strap around my neck I tie the rope to each side of the ladder near the bottom rung. Then I lower myself until the rope is holding me under the arms and the rest of me is dangling into the water. I take a few deep breaths and then lower my head, looking down through the lens. My heart is so loud and fast in my ears that at first I think someone's started a motor nearby.

There are two men in full scuba gear, including wet suits, swimming around our dive site, carefully poking through our staked-out area with poles. They are well lit. Well enough, I hope, for me to get some good shots. They're at the edge of my camera range, but the water is clear and there's a lot of light. I fire away, afraid that the strobe flash from the camera will alert them, but somehow it doesn't. Peripheral vision's not great in a face mask, and they're flooded with their own lights.

I feel the most incredible rage boil in me when I see one of them dig around and then pick something out of the sand, examine it, and put it into a collecting bag. Whatever it is, it's something we did the work for. I take one last shot of them and then go back up the ladder while my luck is holding.

I admit I'm afraid, even as I know they're the ones who should be. If I'd made my presence known, they'd be the ones in trouble. Or I might be, depending on how ruthless and/or impulsive they are. There's no denying they have plenty of nerve and guts. I wonder if I should have enough guts to challenge them, but I know I don't. And I've already wasted a lot of time by being afraid to trust my instincts and call the Marine Patrol when I first saw the lights.

I make the call as fast as I can and tell them what's happening. They sound dubious at first but agree to come out.

Then I wake Nathan and he's furious I didn't wake him earlier.

"Why?" I ask him as I follow him out on deck. "What would you have done that I didn't? I had to be sure something was really happening. Are you going down after them?"

He turns around and gives me a hard look. "We ain't looking to be killed, Brian. We already know they're bad guys—and they could have weapons. But man, I'd like to let them know we know they're there."

"We could," I say. "We could put a light down."

"And scare them away before the patrol arrives? Forget that. We still have a chance to catch them."

He's hopping mad—at them and at me—and I pray for the Marine Patrol to show up and distract him even though I doubt they'll arrive in time to catch our thieves.

And they don't. We see the lights on the patrol boat coming across the black water at about the same time we see the two underwater lights head back toward the

Pelican. By the time the Marine Patrol arrives, the underwater lights are gone and the *Pelican* is dark and quiet.

A guy in an official windbreaker comes aboard.

"So what's going on?" he says. "You the one that called?" he asks Nathan.

Nathan jerks his thumb at me.

"I called," I say. "At first I wasn't sure what was happening, so I took a look—"

Nathan makes a sound like an underground explosion.

I ignore him and go on, "—and saw them down there, two guys in scuba gear and lights, picking through our archaeological site. There wasn't any logical reason for them to be there, and we'd already had a suspicion somebody'd been at the site when we weren't here, so—"

"So you called us," the police guy says.

"Yeah," I say. "But first I took some pictures."

Nathan puts his palm against his forehead and sits down in a deck chair.

The police guy is writing. "Okay," he says. "Then what?"

"Then you came and they went."

"Did you see where they went?" he asks me.

"Yeah," I say and point out to where the *Pelican* was. But it's gone. Somehow it's left without lights and without noise. Maybe the same way it did the night before, if Leo surprised it when he came back in the *Conch.* "Well, there was a boat there," I say. "The *Pelican.* It's been there for a few days pretending to fish."

"What makes you think they're not really fishing?"

he asks me, and I start to feel like some kind of suspect myself.

I glance at Nathan. He's looking at me, paying attention but letting me carry this by myself.

"They watch us," I say.

"Well, that sounds pretty suspicious," he says, and I can't tell if he's being sarcastic or not.

"I have the pictures," I tell him. "I can show you later today."

"Okay," he says. "You do that." He turns to Nathan. "You have anything to say?" he asks.

Nathan shakes his head, then says, "Except that they *have* been watching us. And they've been on our site before. That's why we're out here tonight, keeping watch."

"They or somebody else? You have proof it's them?" This guy is a real pain. I want to remind him that we're the good guys. We're not up at 4 a.m. because we like the way it feels. I remember my talk on the beach with Tia and wonder if they're acting this way because I'm a kid and Nathan's a black man: people they feel they can dismiss. I can see how it wouldn't take long to start getting very paranoid; suspicious that the way people treat you has more to do with you than with the fact that they're jerks.

When neither Nathan nor I speak, he flips his notebook closed and heads for the side. "You bring me those pictures when you get them done and we'll see what shows up."

He climbs down into his idling boat and motors off.

"You took pictures?" Nathan asks me.

I nod.

"Well, you were lucky," he says. "If they'd known you had a camera . . ." He shakes his head. "Lucky and foolish. It's a miracle they didn't see that flash."

"But if the pictures turn out," I say, angry, "we'll have our evidence."

He shakes his head again and stands up. "Well, they better turn out after the risk you took. I know I'm not going to be doing any more sleeping tonight. How about you?"

"No."

"Then how about some breakfast?" he says.

He makes us omelets full of stuff, cheese and mushrooms and peppers. There's a mango and coffee cake and a lot of hot coffee, and we eat for a long time without talking. I quit feeling quite so pushed out of shape. I guess what I did *was* foolish, and I finally figure out Nathan is mad because he was worried. Still, I'd like a *little* credit for trying to do something.

Maybe that's what the sumptuous breakfast is for. Or maybe Nathan just likes to cook.

The *Crazy Conch* arrives about seven-thirty, and Leo, Rafe, and Tia work on what's left of the fruit and cake and coffee while we fill them in.

Leo doesn't say anything and I try to interpret the looks he gives me. Disgust? Contempt? Pity?

The *Pelican* has not reappeared.

"So it looks like we have the day off," Rafe says.

"No," Tia says. "Why?"

"Because Brian and I have to go back to Fortunata and develop pictures."

"But the rest of us can keep going," Tia says.

Rafe shakes his head. "Not without supervision. This

project is my baby, and it's not going to be compromised any more than it already is. You can stay out here if you like. I still want a twenty-four-hour watch. But no diving when I'm gone. However, I think we ought to go down now and take a look."

We hurry into our gear and go. And can't tell a thing. It's not like we're going to find footmarks and fingerprints. And the tide moves things around without any human help. Whatever they've taken is something we hadn't found yet ourselves, so there's no documentation to prove it's missing. That's bad enough. Worse is not knowing what they found or how important it is. Maybe it's the item with the name on it that would prove we had the *Cádiz*.

We come up, disturbed and discouraged. Tia decides to stay out on the water with Leo on the *Conch*. That should make for a quiet afternoon. I bet they could go until tomorrow without talking at all. Nathan wants to come in with Rafe and me so he can get some sleep. We're all resentful at losing a precious day of diving, especially now in hurricane season, when anytime a storm could put us out of business.

TWENTY

By midafternoon Rafe and I have the pictures, and they're worthless. Two masked figures in rubber suits swimming underwater. The light's so good you can hardly even tell it's night. And you definitely can't tell what they're doing. Or who they are.

I throw the pile of photos on the counter in Lisbon's bathroom darkroom. "There's no point in taking these to the Marine Patrol," I say.

"But we will," Rafe says. "If only to prove that our complaint isn't frivolous. Let's go."

It's no surprise that the Marine Patrol don't get excited about our pictures. They say they'll keep them on file and let us know if there are any developments. We know what that means. They tell us they've located the *Pelican* and it's just some guys on vacation, fishing and diving.

Right.

We leave the police station feeling low. The air is as hot as ever and heavy as mud. There seems to be a greenish tinge to the sky, and I wonder if exhaustion is making me hallucinate.

Rafe looks up, too. "Storm coming," he says. "Pretty far off still. Maybe it'll miss us."

We drive back to Fortunata and stop at Nathan's. He's up, but just, standing in the kitchen with a glass of iced tea in his hand.

When we tell him what's happened at the station, he puts his hand on my shoulder. "Nice try," he says, and I wonder if he still thinks I'm foolish.

"I'm going out now to relieve Leo and Tia," Rafe says. "I'll stay out there tonight."

"So will I," I say. I don't want to be anywhere with Leo tonight either at home or on the water. I believe he'll let me know what he thinks about my performance last night even if he doesn't use many words. Besides, I feel as if I have to atone somehow for not catching the thieves. Maybe if I'd called the Marine Patrol sooner, we could have.

"No," Rafe says. "You were there last night. You're tired."

"Not that tired," I say, "and I promise not to do anything stupid. Please let me go. Nathan can sleep tonight. He and Leo can stay out there tomorrow night."

"You sure?" Rafe asks. I nod. "Okay, then."

He and I go out and send Leo and Tia back on the *Crazy Conch*. I'm so tired I'm almost staggering, but I won't tell Rafe and he's too preoccupied with his missed day of diving and the storm on the weather reports and his worries about the *Pelican* to pay much attention to me. Except to tell me that his shark oil's a little cloudy and we should expect some rain. We've already heard that on the weather report, so I'm not giving shark oil much credit.

Rafe's not the cook that Nathan is, but he's a better checkers player. He decides to try to teach me chess, but I don't seem to have the mind for it. Or maybe I would if I wasn't so tired. To keep myself awake, I ask him to tell me stories about his work.

Finally he sweeps the chess pieces into their box and says, "Why don't we just get some sodas and you unload all the questions you want?"

"How about cappuccinos? I'll make them." Nathan's gourmetness has seriously impressed me. I like the idea of being a great cook, even if, in this case, all it means is boiling water for the ready-mix coffee. I can still sprinkle cinnamon and chocolate on the top and make it look like a much bigger deal than it actually is.

We sit in the stern, bobbing and rocking softly, the air stirred by enough of an offshore breeze to relieve the oppressive heat. The running lights are on, but in the great black of sea and sky they don't look like much. The moon appears and disappears between the clouds, making a path on the water that I imagine penetrates clear down to the sand beneath, glinting off my shooting stand, our markers, maybe off treasure unburied by sands that have shifted since we came up this morning. There seems to be a conspiracy out here between sky and sea that makes them part of each other. In the glare of midday it's hard to find the horizon, the dividing line between one and the other. From thirty feet underwater, I can look up and see clouds.

"Okay, shoot," Rafe says.

"Have you even been in real danger underwater?"

"Oh, sure," he says. "Mostly through my own stupidity and carelessness—diving alone, running out of air, that kind of stuff. I'm a lot more careful now than when I was younger and thought I was bulletproof."

"But what about sharks and octopuses and nitrogen narcosis?"

He laughs. "That's Hollywood, not reality. Octopi are really too shy to give you trouble. They hide or make an ink cloud. Nitrogen narcosis is only a problem at a hundred feet or more, and I don't like to dive that deep. You spend more time going up and down, decompressing, than you do on the bottom. It's boring. Sharks can be a problem, but we're usually making so much noise with the compressor or the air lift or the drills that they stay away. Hey, don't look so disappointed. Were you hoping for some emergencies besides thieves?"

"Well, you know. A little excitement."

"What, finding a three-hundred-and-fifty-year-old ship's not exciting enough for you? That's supposed to be the good part."

"Oh, I like that," I say. "A lot. I was just wondering."

"I get it," he says. "More war stories to tell when you get home. Well, if we're lucky, you could have your picture in the paper and on TV. But, you know, this is work you have to do because you like it, not for the glory, because there's a whole lot more work than glory to it. As we archaeologists say, our profession is mostly moving dirt." He pauses. "You'd be a good archaeologist, Brian," he says. "You're careful and tenacious and find ways to keep yourself from getting bored when it seems like all we're doing is rearranging the bottom of the channel."

"Yeah?" With everything else he has to do, running the search, he's found time to watch me. I feel like some kind of community experiment being monitored by a bunch of people who each want a different result. Nathan wants me to become some kind of SuperGoodMan; Tia wants . . . well, something, but I don't know what it is; Leo wants me to disappear; and now Rafe wants me to turn into an archaeologist.

Actually, it isn't such a bad idea. Everything I like is involved in it. Scuba, photography, computers, hanging out with interesting people, the puzzle of the unknown. Maybe Rafe has put me onto something; one more thing Tia can resent. And given me what Nathan says I need: another good man to imitate.

"Well," I say, "it's something to think about."

"Most everything is," he says.

We watch the night for a while, the clouds and the moon playing games, until I'm falling asleep in my chair.

"Go to bed," Rafe says. "No *Pelican* yet and I'm betting we won't see her tonight; not after our visit from the patrol last night."

"You think they're gone for good?" I ask, levering myself up.

"Maybe. Depends on how greedy they are. We'll find out."

TWENTY-ONE

It's daylight when I wake, a dirty gray daylight that's barely lighting the cabin, and there's the sound of serious rain on the deck. I roll out of bed, noting that the other bunk is made but the pillow's dented, as if someone had slept on top of the covers. I stagger for balance on a boat that's rocking as if it's in a washing machine.

Rafe's in the galley. The stove's on gimbals and has rails all around it to keep pots from sliding off, but cooking in this high a sea isn't a great idea. He doesn't think so either. He's braced in the corner of a bench, shoveling cold cereal into his mouth. I join him and do the same.

"You didn't wake me," I say. "Did you watch all night?"

"Nah," he says. "I set my alarm every hour and took a look, but mostly I slept. The *Pelican* never showed. Weather's too dirty for crime, I guess."

"Is this going to be a hurricane?" I ask.

"Somewhere, maybe," he says, "but not here. Here it's just a plain old rainstorm with thunder and lightning and all the special effects."

"Have you ever been in a hurricane?" I ask. "What's it like?"

"Bad," he says. "I hope you never see one. I hope none of us see one this summer."

I pray this storm isn't making the news in whatever city Mom is in now. If it is, she'll be on the phone, panicky and unreasonable, and I don't want to hear about it.

"Can we dive today?" I think I know the answer, but I ask anyway.

"We could," he says. "It's probably quiet enough down there. But it would be difficult up here, so we won't. What I will do is dismantle the shooting stand, as a precaution against the weather." I hear the frustration in his voice—another day lost. "I talked to Nathan by radio already."

"So we're staying out here?"

He gets up, rinses his bowl in the sink, dries it, and puts it away in a latched cupboard. "Just me, not you. You get the day off. Nathan's volunteered to come back out with me when I bring the *Angelfish* in. The *Pelican*'s lying low, but we don't want to take any chances. Those guys are sneaky. Let's hope things are quieter tomorrow." He sighs. "There's plenty of paperwork I can do."

By the time we get the *Angelfish* in, moored, and buttoned down, it's close to noon, still raining like crazy, still hot, and so humid I feel like I'm underwater without tanks. We're already soaked, so we're in no big rush to get inside. I walk with Rafe to the End of the Rainbow. With his wild ginger hair and beard flattened by the rain, he looks like a wet haystack.

He catches me grinning at him. "Well, you don't look like any *GQ* guy yourself," he says, and then we're laughing like maniacs while the rain pours down on us. He grabs me around the neck and wrestles me over onto the grass in front of Lisbon's. We're rolling around, laughing and growling, and trying to push each other's faces into the mud, when we hear Tia's voice from the porch.

"Now, that's something you'd never see two women doing."

I sit up, filthy and sheepish. Maybe it was tension relief, maybe it was high spirits, maybe it was typical loutish male behavior—all I know is that it felt great, wrestling in the rain with a guy I like and respect and who has maybe handed me my future.

Now, thanks to Tia, I feel like a little boy who's been caught doing something he shouldn't.

"Ah, give it a rest, Tia," Rafe says, leaning back on his hands and grinning. Now he looks like a wet haystack that's been rearranged by a tractor. "You'll never see us going recreational shoe-shopping either, the way women do. We're two different species. That's what makes it interesting."

I can see I should have talked to Rafe before I took seriously Tia's contention that men have no reason for being. Right now, wrestling in the rain seems like enough reason for being to me.

I expect to hear her make some rude response, but instead she laughs. I realize it's the first time I've heard her do that, and it's a sound almost as good as Lisbon's laugh. "Maybe you're right," she says. "Were you thinking of coming in the house that way?"

"Unless you'd like us to strip out here on the lawn—something I'm sure you think we're likely to do anyway," Rafe says.

She laughs again. What's happened to my edgy, fractious Tia? "I'll bring you some towels," she says.

We take hot showers and I put on some of Rafe's odd clothes, which are much too big and make me feel as if I'm masquerading as somebody bigger, wiser, and less fashion-hip than I am. Lisbon makes us hot chocolate, which seems strange considering the tropical steaminess outside, but it tastes great. I don't want to go home to Leo, but finally, when Rafe goes off to get Nathan, I have to get on my feet.

"Wait," Tia says. "I'll get an umbrella and walk with you."

Outside, the sky seems a little lighter and the rain is slackening some.

"You're in a good mood," I say. "What's wrong?"

"Well, thank you very much," she says. "Never mind. I just feel fine for some reason." She gives me a sidelong look. "I don't know why. Is that okay with you?"

"Be my guest."

"You want to do something tonight?" she asks.

I try to hide my surprise. I don't want to do anything to scare off this new, friendlier Tia. "Like what? Dinner at Captain Hook's?"

"God, no," she says, making a face. "They *should* apologize in advance. Let's go down to Key West, get us a few conch fritters or a lot of Cuban food and listen to some music. Maybe I'll teach you to kissy-boogie."

I'm not even going to ask what that is. "Isn't Key West a long way from here?" I remember a couple of trips down there with Leo when I was a kid, and it seems to me that they took forever.

"About forty miles."

"Over little bridges in the rain and the dark, the way you drive? Sure, why not," I say.

She elbows me. "Is this the hero of the *Pelican* incident talking?"

"There isn't anyone who thinks I was a hero," I say. "Nathan thinks I was stupid, and the Marine Patrol think I'm imagining it, and Rafe's annoyed at missing a good day of diving, and Leo didn't even talk to me."

We splash along for a few steps and she says, "I think you were a hero."

I look at her to be sure she's serious. "You do?"

"Well, you tried to get a picture of them. Without that, there wouldn't be any proof at all."

"Turns out there isn't, anyway."

"But," she insists, "you didn't know the pictures wouldn't show anything. You *tried*. Isn't that the part you think is the most important?"

Did I say that? I decide to quit arguing with her. It feels too good to be vindicated. "What time do you want to leave?" I ask.

"As soon as you get on some clothes that match. Not to mention fit."

Leo's at the kitchen table smoking when we come in. He looks surprised to see us.

"Rafe and I came in and he and Nathan went out again," I say. "No sign of the *Pelican* while we were out there."

"Okay," he says.

Tia sits down at the table with him and gives me a dismissive gesture. "Go get changed," she says. "I'll keep Leo company." As I go, I hear her telling Leo we're going to Key West.

"Be careful on the road," he says, sounding strangely like a parent.

When I return, dressed, Tia stands and gives me an approving nod. "Much better," she says.

Leo gets up and walks with us to the door. Tia has already gone down the steps when he gives me a small punch in the shoulder and says, "Too bad about the coins."

"Yeah," I say, stopping. I wait for him to go on, to blame me. It seems as if he's waiting for something, too. After an awkward moment, I continue down the steps.

"Have a good time," he says.

"Yeah," I say again.

TWENTY-TWO

The trip isn't as bad as I expect. Tia drives slower than she did going to Marathon, and I wonder how much of that performance was to shake me up. There's still daylight, the rain is tapering off, and there's no traffic. We sing with the radio all the way down and argue about the bands we like. We agree on Pearl Jam. Then we argue about what their name means. I think it's either a total nonsense combination of words or a jam session so perfect it's like a pearl. She thinks it's stuff to spread on your bread made of crushed pearls—sort of food for the gods.

Tia drives me around Key West pointing things out: the topless beach, Hemingway's house, a bar with the motto "See the Lower Keys on Your Hands and Knees," a voodoo shop, the southernmost point in the continental United States, Mallory Square and its tourist traps, and Mel Fisher's treasure exhibit, which, unfortunately, is closed. I'd like to see some examples of what we might yet find.

I feel like a hick from the sticks already after only a few weeks in Fortunata, and all these urban-Key sights seem exciting, even in the rain. Of course, the excitement could be partly due to the company. She's infuriating, confusing, stubborn, and obnoxious, it's true, but she's still exciting to be with.

At dusk—too cloudy for a sunset tonight—we end up at a little Cuban place off Duval Street where we eat shredded pork and black beans and a strange kind of melon next to a window open wide to the soft, damp evening. The service is just neglectful enough.

"This was a good idea," I say.

"Key West is a pretty odd place," she says, "but it suits how I've been feeling the past couple of days— kind of confused and undecided but lighthearted anyhow."

I don't know what to say about that, so I just give her a clumsy pat on the arm—and notice that the color contrast between our skins is less than it was; I've gotten tan.

"You think we'll find the *Cádiz?*" I ask.

She waves her hand. "Of course. We're already finding it. And as soon as we have proof that it's really the *Cádiz*, we can announce it. It's probably too bad it wasn't a whole lot harder—makes us think it's always this easy. Not that I'm complaining. It's nice to have something be even slightly easy for a change."

"Well, Rafe did his homework first. All digs would probably be easy if you knew exactly where to look."

"I'm sure Nathan would have something instructive to say about that—like the value of careful preparation."

"You'll have his voice in your head the rest of your life," I say.

She makes a face. "You're right. Sometimes I'd like to gag that voice. I always know just what he'd say about something I'm doing, and I don't always like it. And sometimes I plain don't care."

"What would he say about us having dinner?"

"It would concern him, the black-and-white thing. He'd like it better if I kept to black guys. But he knows there are too few here, and that I'm not going to do without a social life. But I know he thinks you could be a good influence on me, which should make me hate you, so maybe he thinks it's safe for us to be together. You the good example and me the problem. Don't think I haven't noticed that he's made you his Boy Scout. Soon he'll be pushing on you as hard as he does on me."

"He already is. It's not my idea, you know, to be a good example."

"That's a relief," she says with a Mona Lisa smile. "You want to be bad, like me?"

"I don't think you're bad," I say. "I think you're fine."

"What about how being with me is like carrying something heavy uphill? What about how I'm no picnic?"

"All true," I say, not excusing her. "But you're working on some big stuff. There's a possibility that you'll improve." I'm kidding her now, and I hope she knows it.

She does. "Oh, your missionary work must be so rewarding," she says in her sincere voice.

Modestly, I look at my plate. "I hate to brag about it," I say, and she laughs.

We go someplace else, a place that looks like an ice-cream parlor, but with a band, and we listen to the music and she teaches me to kissy-boogie. It can be as raunchy as you want it to be, or as athletic, and somehow I can imagine Lisbon and Nathan doing it in the kitchen and laughing. I wish I could imagine Mom and the Guy doing it.

It's late when we head back, but the air is clean and cool and the flying teeth are temporarily blown to Cuba. The moonlight flickering through breaking clouds gives a fairy-dust luster to the landscape as we drive back up the Keys, flashing over bridges, past mangrove swamps and tourist clutter, buttonwood sloughs and telephone poles, and everywhere the gleam and glitter and glide of water. There is an other-worldly quality to this whole trip and I feel a little like I did this afternoon in Rafe's clothing—like someone other than who I am. Or who I used to think I was.

We don't talk; just watch the moon-drenched waterscape and listen to the music on the radio.

Tia stops at Leo's and turns off the motor, but doesn't say anything. We sit in silence for a while and then, as if some signal has been given, we lean toward each other. I know she knows what she's doing and I don't, but as soon as our mouths meet, it doesn't make any difference. Instinct takes over. I try to keep my brain working, but other parts of my body are drowning it out. Probably a good thing, because my brain is saying, "Stop, stupid!"

We come up for air and I put my hands on her shoulders. I'm the one who's hearing Nathan's voice loud in my ear now.

"What?" she asks.

"Are we going to be sorry about this tomorrow?"

"We could find out," she says, always willing to take a risk. "You're the one who told me I should pick something—anything—and get involved with it."

I turn away from her and look out the window. "Thanks. Being just 'anything' is very flattering."

She makes an annoyed sound. "That's not what I meant." She exhales noisily. "Honestly. The male ego."

I think of a bunch of things I could say, like, "Females don't have egos?" or "So what *did* you mean?" or "Okay, let's find out," but none of them seem right, so I keep quiet.

"Oh, come on," she says, taking my arm. "Things were going so well."

"You think so?" I ask. Here's that anger again, out of nowhere. I point it at her, but I'm not sure that's where it should be going. It doesn't matter: I can't shut myself up. "Well, why wouldn't you? As long as you're getting your way, as long as everybody's fussing over and worrying about and concentrating on you, I guess things do seem to be going well. And it's a lot easier to be the problem and then sit back while everybody else tries to make it better than it is to get up off your butt and change anything yourself."

"Hey," she says and pushes my shoulder.

I face her. "Of course you wouldn't look at it that way, but maybe you should try it."

"Get out of the car," she says.

I open the door. I'm tired of difficult people; I want

to be with Nathan and Lisbon, or even Rafe, not Tia or Leo: I want to be with people who are taking care of their own business without letting it slop over onto other people.

I get out of the car and lean back in. "Just for the record," I say, "this has nothing to do with what color you are. I don't care if you're black or white or both or neither. Don't you know everybody feels like an outsider in some way? What your biggest problem is, is you're difficult. Why don't you work on that one?" I walk away without closing the car door, but I hear it slam behind me and the tires of Lisbon's car kick up gravel as Tia guns the motor and roars out of the drive.

The cottage is completely dark. Leo knows I'm out, and it never even occurs to him to leave a light on for me.

TWENTY-THREE

Tia and I ride out with Leo in the *Crazy Conch* the next morning, but I don't want to speak to either one of them. Apparently, it's mutual, as they make no attempts to engage me in conversation either. I just wish Tia didn't look so good, standing in the bow with the wind blowing her curls around like streamers.

When we rendezvous, it seems that the days off and the threat of the *Pelican*, which is still absent, have filled Rafe with a strong resolve. He even passes out T-shirts to us that say NO WEENIES! I set the camera on auto and run so I can get into the picture of us, with our arms up and our mouths open, yelling, "No weenies!"

I wonder if the picture can possibly show all the complications that flow between and among us. Sometimes these things do seem to show in photographs, and other times faces can be so treacherous, hiding everything important.

In spite of Rafe's enthusiasm, it's a discouraging day. The site is a mess from the storm surge, and we have to reestablish our grids and reset the shooting stand. And move acres of sand around just trying to get back to where we were, forget about making any progress.

The *Pelican* shows up for a while in the afternoon, fishing gear prominently in action, and then goes in before we do. Maybe they can tell we're having no luck.

Nathan and Leo stay out on the *Angelfish* while Rafe, Tia, and I go back on the *Crazy Conch*. I drive while Rafe rattles his computer printouts and mutters over them, and Tia stays as far away from me as she can.

When we dock, I say, "Go on. I'll button things up." I want them to leave me alone. I don't want to talk to anybody. I've spent the whole day being cooperative and agreeable, and I don't want to do that anymore.

Rafe nods absentmindedly, scoops his piles of papers into his briefcase, and heads off, preoccupied, while I go down to straighten up the galley. I'm standing with a dish towel in one hand and a bouquet of silverware in the other when I sense I'm not alone.

I turn around and there's Tia on the steps, looking down at me. I don't say anything. I figure I've already had my say. It's her move now.

We face each other for what seems like a long time, waiting. I'm about to go back to my domestic chores when she says, "Pay attention," in a commanding tone of voice.

"All right," I say. I put down the silver and the towel and stick my hands in my back pockets.

"I don't say this very often, so I'm only going to say it once." She stops as if she can't bring herself to say it even once. She clears her throat and says, very softly, "I'm sorry. I know sometimes I can be such a witch, or something that sounds like that. Although I have to say, I don't think I was so bad last night, so is there something else bothering you?"

I think for a minute. I want to get this right. Then I say, "I don't know. Maybe. But even so, what's going on between you and me stays the same. I can understand some of what's bothering you, but it's still not okay to act the way you do, that silent, bratty, rude stuff. Everybody's got problems. It's not permission to be that word that sounds like witch."

Then I realize I'd better respond to the important part, and add, "But I believe you're sorry for hurting me, or offending me, or whatever I was. Thanks for the apology."

Her mouth relaxes a little. "Do you think maybe we could start over, pretend we're just meeting for the first time?"

"No. Anyway, I don't want to forget everything. Last night in Key West was fun, and I'm glad you got me *Red Sky at Morning.*"

Her face brightens. "Did you laugh out loud?"

"Yeah. 'Hunnert percent,' " I say, quoting a joke from the book.

She almost laughs. "Did you cry at the end?"

"Not quite."

"That's good enough. What about *Red Badge of Courage?*"

"Haven't read it yet. I'll let you know when I do."

She sits down on the step. "You're probably right," she says. "Mama and Nathan lean on me a lot, but they give me a lot of rope, too. Maybe too much."

"Maybe," I say. "I can shorten it for you."

"Might be better if I learn how to do that for myself."

"Yeah," I say. "What made you decide to?"

She hunches her shoulders and crosses her arms, sticking her hands in her armpits. "Watching myself drive somebody away. It came to me that maybe people don't always leave for mysterious reasons, or for reasons of color. That the way you act with them might have something to do with it."

"Who?" I ask.

"You, you dummy," she says and then puts her hand over her mouth. "Whoops. This isn't going to be easy," she says, "but it's a project I should get involved in, I guess." She waits for me to say something, but nothing occurs to me, so she goes on, "No matter what I do, I know Mama and Nathan aren't going anywhere. They might not like the way I'm acting—I *know* they don't—but they'll wait me out, and Nathan, especially, doesn't have to. So the people who really care stay if they can." She sighs. "It's not my fault my father disappeared, but it might be my fault if other people do."

People stay if they can. I've always thought Leo hasn't stayed, but that's not really true. He's stayed in the sense that he's there waiting for me every summer, he's never canceled a visit, he always lets me know when he moves. It would have been easy for him to vanish like Tia's dad, but he hasn't. But how much does that mean? It's so meager.

She sticks out her hand. "Friends?" When she sees

me hesitate, she hastily says, "How about pre-friends? Friends in training? Not the instant kind but the made-from-scratch kind, the hard way?"

I take her hand. "Hard is right," I say.

With unfamiliar modesty she says, shyly, "Maybe it'll be worth it."

TWENTY-FOUR

The next week or so we dive all day, finding an impressive heap of shipboard artifacts and tools, a few jewels and more *reales de á ocho*, though nothing that positively identifies the *Cádiz*. It doesn't matter; by now we're all sure it's here—we only have to dig around enough and we'll find it. It's true, there are moments of great frustration, as when Leo brings up an inscribed silver shaving mug with initials on it that match the initials of one of the *Cádiz*'s passengers—and probably hundreds of other people alive in 1648. We *know* it comes from the *Cádiz*, but that's not good enough for science.

I spend my days looking—through a face mask or a camera lens—and I begin to think I can see what isn't visible: thoughts and emotions. I can tell what Rafe is feeling when I see him drop the air lift—whether it's in frustration or in excitement. I can tell what Nathan's thinking when he studies a squall line on the horizon, before he brings out the tarps. It's true what somebody once said: you can observe a lot just by looking.

Except with Leo. Leo remains a shuttered mystery. He works hard and speaks little. Once, when I come home from developing film at Lisbon's, PeeWee's at the cottage with Leo, watching TV. I have no idea what to make of that. Only once do he and I stay out on the *Angelfish* overnight, and we play many hands of gin rummy. He also teaches me about twelve kinds of solitaire. I don't like to think of how many games of that he must have played.

The *Pelican* is still around, but not every day. One night, when Tia and Nathan stay out on the boat, they think they see underwater lights approaching. They respond by aiming a big underwater spot where they see the lights, and the lights go out. Maybe a moonlight mirage, Nathan says. Baloney, Tia says.

Tia and I spend a lot of time together underwater. It's easier there where speech is not required and where we know what we're doing. Rafe comments on how many pictures I take of her, but leaves it at that, for which I'm grateful.

We also spend time on dry land and it goes okay. Tia is careful with me and I can see the strain on her. I would never tell her so, but I miss some of the old sass and vinegar. There's been no more kissing, either. Evidently, that's too advanced for pre-friends. I miss that, too.

I've been in Florida for more than a month now, and

it's like no other visit. For one thing, I have a lot to do, so the time goes fast; for another, I'm not lonely, the way I am with only Leo to be with. And finally, I'm having fun, which has never happened before. I haven't counted the days until I can go home. Now I want them to last longer.

It's a Friday afternoon and we've been following hurricane information on the radio. For three days there's been one building in the Caribbean, the first of the season, Hurricane Angie, and it's as indecisive and fitful as a petulant child, changing direction, stalling, perplexing the meteorologists. We're on Hurricane Watch, which means keep doing what you're doing, but know that a change in the weather could come within twenty-four hours. We watch the sky, which is gray, the water, which is choppy, and the wind, which is erratic, and can't decide what to do.

Rafe is in a hurry now. It's the end of July, hurricane season, his money's running out, and he needs to find proof that we've got the *Cádiz*. He's also a careful guy. But only gamblers at heart go looking for buried treasure in the first place, so he makes the decision I know he's going to.

"Okay, let's leave the *Conch* out here tonight. It could be a mistake, but I'm gambling Angie'll stay in the Caribbean huffing and puffing, or blow out before she gets to us. This would be just the night the *Pelican* guys'd come over if they see we've gone in. Who wants to take the duty?"

"I will," Leo and I say simultaneously.

I say it because I think Rafe is going to volunteer—

his hunt, his risk—and I want another night with him. I don't know why Leo volunteers.

"Fine," Rafe says. "I'll leave you my shark oil just for luck."

And so we're stuck with each other.

TWENTY-FIVE

Leo and I watch the *Angelfish* head back to Fortunata, its wake fragmented by the rain which has begun falling on the turbulent sea.

The sky is now the color of a new bruise and the wind is strong and fitful, boxing the compass.

We leave the radio on, though the reception crackles and fizzes, but the weather reports still say that the storm will miss us by a good margin. Leo turns it down until it's a mutter in the background and says, "You interested in some dinner?"

"Sure. There's stew or chili." Both canned, but Leo's favorite kitchen utensil is the can opener. "What do you want?"

"I'll cook. You can clean up. You're better at that than I am." No joke, I think. "How about the stew?"

"Fine." I stay in the wheelhouse while he goes to the

galley. Rafe's shark oil is cloudy and, I think, ominous.

I sit on a high stool, looking out at the weather, hoping Leo's not making too big a mess of the little galley. And suddenly I'm furious, with that mysterious anger.

Why is he such a slob? Is taking the trash out and washing the dishes such a hard thing? I hate the way he eats so fast and the way he never ties his shoes and the way he's so secretive about his comings and goings. And why does he still smoke when everybody else is quitting?

I also know these are little things and that they're not why I'm so mad. What I'm really angry about is that he is who he is. I want him to be different. I know it drives Tia nuts the way Nathan is with her, but it means something. Why can't Leo pay that kind of attention to me?

I realize I'm going to have to be very careful with myself tonight if I want to avoid some kind of face-off with him.

"Soup's on," he hollers from the galley. That's another thing I hate, I decide. Why can't he say, "Dinner's ready," or "Come to the table," or *anything* besides "Soup's on"? And does he have to yell? I'm not that far away.

I slide onto the bench in the galley as Leo plops two bowls of stew onto the table. The bowls have rubber bottoms so they stay put even though the boat's rocking. And once I'm belowdeck, sitting, I really notice how much it is.

"Aim that spoon with care," Leo says. "Be easy to miss your mouth in a sea like this one."

"There's no way the *Pelican*'s coming out here in this," I say.

"Probably not," he says. "But Rafe wants us out here, so here we are."

"You really think the storm'll pass us?" I ask. "It's raining pretty good."

He shrugs and shovels a spoonful of stew into his mouth. Then, chewing fast and swallowing, he says, "Storms are tricky around here. Unpredictable. Chances are it'll miss us, but you never know."

"What if it hits?"

He shrugs again. "We'll do what we can do."

I'm not crazy about this fatalism. I need to be sure he can take charge so nothing happens to us or the *Conch*. He's not putting my mind at ease.

"I'm not kidding. What if it hits?" I can hear the anger in my voice, so he must be able to.

He chews, then leans back, swaying roughly behind the table. "First we put on life jackets. Then we raise the anchors, start the engine, and try to ride it out." A gust of rain hits the side of the *Conch* with the sound of buckshot. "If we're lucky, we'll make it."

I can't eat. The stew is only lukewarm and not that good to start with. I stand, and sway as the boat rolls under me. I put my hand on the bulkhead for support. "What if we're not lucky?"

He's eating again. "They say drowning's a very peaceful death."

I imagine the moment of having to take an underwater breath, lungs bursting for oxygen, and choking on tons of seawater. How is that supposed to be peaceful?

"You'd let us drown?" I almost scream. "Let's pull up the anchors now! Let's go in now! Why should we wait?"

"We're safer out here than in an anchorage where we can get bashed to pieces against the dock. Smart boat owners always put out in a storm if they can't get to a safe anchorage." Then, as if to himself, he says, "There were times I'd have welcomed a peaceful death." He looks up, at me, and says, "I'll keep things under control. You go to bed."

"*You're* going to keep things under control?" I can't keep the scorn out of my voice. When has he ever had things under control? Putting out to sea in a hurricane doesn't sound so smart to me.

"Yes," he says calmly. "I know how to do that. On a boat."

"Not anywhere else," I say. I press my lips together to keep myself from saying more of the angry things that are so close to the surface now.

"Maybe not," he says. He doesn't sound outraged, the way I would have thought, or even surprised.

I stand, looking at him, my fists clenched. Can I trust him? I don't know. And that seems a terrible admission to make about my own father.

I jerk away from the table and him and run, throwing myself into the forward section and onto the bunk. I pull the sheet up over me and, though I don't expect to, I fall asleep.

He's shaking me. "Brian, Brian," he's saying urgently.

"Huh?" I say, startled, sitting up so fast my head swims.

"The hurricane's changed course. We've got to get moving."

I'm on my feet, almost sick to my stomach with fear.

I follow him. He yanks open a locker and hands me a life vest. "Put that on and get ready to get those anchors up. And kiss the *Nueva Cádiz* goodbye."

"Why? What do you mean?" I struggle into my life vest.

"I mean that even if the leading edge of the hurricane misses us, there'll be enough turbulence down there to rip out all our markers and cover that site with tons of sand."

"Or uncover parts we haven't gotten to," I say. "Why do you have to be so negative?"

Rain rattles violently against the windows, flooding them. I can't see out. The *Conch* rocks and wallows, and it seems to me that if we wait a minute, the anchors will pull themselves up.

"In my experience," he said, "the negative is what you're more likely to get." He's standing with his life vest in his hand. He seems to be slowing down, even as the need for speed overcomes me.

"Well, not in mine. Maybe you get what you expect. Or deserve." It occurs to me that without the anchors out, the *Conch* will have no defense against the sea. "Are you sure we should bring up the anchors? Aren't we safer anchored?"

"For a while, yeah," he says. "But we've got no maneuverability if it gets worse than this. We could be swamped without a chance." To my relief, he puts on his life vest and opens the door to the deck.

Wind-driven rain hits us like a blow, driving him back into me. It's the most physical contact I can ever remember having with him. We put our heads down and push out into the tempest. Instantly my hair is plastered to my head and rivers of water run into my eyes.

What I'm not prepared for is the noise. A heaving sea is a living thing, groaning and roaring. The wind screams and the rain falls in heavy sheets, striking the deck like pebbles. I can barely see the running lights through the curtain of rain and wind-blown sea.

The first anchor is winching up, banging against the hull as it comes. If it ruptures the *Conch*'s side, we'll have a whole new problem to worry about.

The deck is pitching and awash and our bare feet aren't enough traction. I slide and slip, grabbing on to stanchions and railings for support. Leo and I crash against each other as we start bringing in the second anchor. Then he staggers back to the helm house, where he's left the wheel secured. Someone needs to be steering now, and while I don't want it to be me, I'm not sure I want it to be him, either.

By the time I get the anchors up and reach the helm house, Leo is standing, legs apart and braced, wrestling with the wheel, turning us into the wind. The radio is on, but we can hardly hear it over the crash of the sea—only a disconnected phrase now and again: ". . . bridges clogged with traffic . . . winds of seventy to eighty miles an hour . . . Category One hurricane . . ."

I hang on and watch Leo wrestle with the wheel. Eventually he yells at me to take the wheel, and when I do, he slumps forward, his back and upper arms cramping with effort.

The wheel bucks in my hands as if it's alive, and I can barely hold on to it. Then I understand why Leo's muscles are in spasm and grudgingly admire his tenacity.

For hours we struggle in turns at the wheel, fighting the increasing wind and sea, listening to things below crash and fall. Visibility is nil, and all we want to do is stay afloat and ride it out. My mind is full of the kind of prayers I heard at Lisbon's dinner table: plainspoken and heartfelt.

We don't speak. When a wave crashes over the boat, or lifts us in a crazy lurch, one of us might make a sound, the kind of involuntary sound that can't be duplicated on a sunny day on dry land.

I'm bruised on parts of my body I'd forgotten I have from being thrown around by the storm, and my mouth is dry with fear.

The boat lifts, tilting at such an angle that it seems impossible we won't capsize into the boiling sea. Somehow, just as it seems we must fall, the *Conch* rights herself, and we go back to fighting the storm, spelling each other at shortening intervals as we tire.

After an immeasurable time, imperceptibly at first, and then more noticeably, the wind backs off. Though still strong, the rage seems gone from it, like a wild animal exhausted from a frenzy of killing. I feel it first in my arms, bonded to the wheel, before my brain recognizes it.

"Eye of the storm?" I ask.

"I doubt the whole hurricane came this far so fast. It's probably the edge that hit us and now is passing on. We'll know soon." He fiddles with the radio, but all we get is static.

The floor is wet with rain and sea that no door or window is sealed tight enough to keep out, and we slide as the boat rises and drops, trying to hold our balance.

The shriek of the wind drops a bit more and I begin

to feel hopeful. Maybe I will live to be seventeen after all. I relax my grip on the wheel slightly, easing my sore muscles. And as I do that, the boat swerves a little to port, just as a monster wave from nowhere—not that I could have seen it coming anyway, through the streaming windows—hits the *Conch* broadside and a wall of water crashes against the door, bursting it open, and floods into the wheelhouse.

TWENTY-SIX

I'm upside down in cold water, thrown against walls or floor, I can't tell. My head slams against something and my ears ring from the blow. Corners of something else dig into my back and sides. Though I scrabble with my hands, I can't grasp anything to keep me from being thrown around by the water. I hold my breath until I'm dizzy, afraid past imagining of taking that watery breath.

I can feel the wave withdrawing, pulling me with it, and I'm helpless against it. I know I'll be sucked through the open door in the rush of water, and carried over the side.

A hand closes around my ankle, and for a moment the pull of the water equals the strength of the hand. Then the water retreats and I lie on the floor of the wheelhouse, gasping and choking, my left arm flung crookedly over my head, my father's hand still tight around my ankle.

I can hear him coughing, too. I move my head, which rings and aches and spins, to look behind me. Leo is on his knees, one arm hooked through the wheel spokes, blood from a cut on his forehead leaking into his eyes, diluted by the water streaming from his hair. Painfully, he disengages his arm from the wheel, still holding on to me with his other hand.

"Brian?" he says. "Bri? Are you okay?"

I've always wondered why people say that in situations where everything is clearly *not* okay. A more appropriate question is "Are you alive?" or "Are your brains still working?" but nobody ever says that.

I gave the answer people usually give, the answer that means "Yes, I'm still alive."

"I'm fine," I say, with my eyes so swollen I can hardly see out of them, my head vibrating, my body hurting everywhere, a lot more in some places than others; places I'm not sure I'll be having the use of anytime soon. "How about you?"

"Fine," he says, wiping blood out of his eyes with his free hand.

The *Conch* with no one at the wheel tosses on the waves, rainwater still floods against the windows, the door flops and bangs as seawater sloshes back and forth across the floor and me.

We're fine.

"Stay there," Leo says, as if I can go anywhere. He finally releases my ankle and levers himself upright. He secures the wheel and then the door and then kneels beside me, bracing himself with one hand against the bulkhead. "God," he says when he's given me a good look. It doesn't make me feel better.

"My arm hurts," I say.

"No wonder," he says. "I don't think it's supposed to bend that way. Can you sit up?"

He takes me by the shoulders and helps me to sit. My arm throbs more than any other part of me, but it's a close race with my head.

He gets to his feet and gently helps me to mine. When I'm on my feet, he backs me into a corner and picks up the high-backed stool that the monster wave has thrown around the wheelhouse. I'm sure some of my bruises match the shapes of parts of that stool. He braces me more firmly into the corner with the stool.

"I'll be right back," he says.

"Wait!" I say. There are more waves out there that can come after me again, and I'm in poorer shape to resist another one than the last one, which I haven't done all that well with anyway.

But he's gone out the door, which he makes sure is closed tight, into the downpour. Not that it makes much difference, since he's already soaked.

In a few minutes, long ones for me, he's back with the first-aid kit, a blanket, which he wraps around me, and a pillowcase. The pillowcase he tears into pieces to make a sling for my left arm, which by now is swelling alarmingly. The sling doesn't make my arm feel any better but at least reminds me not to use it, which I keep trying to do, activating the pain all over again.

We patch each other's worst cuts with antiseptic cream and Band-Aids, lurching and pitching with the roll of the sea. It might have been funny, I guess, if we'd been watching it instead of doing it. Doing it hurts.

Somehow the radio is working again. ". . . passing on to the north and east. Damage reports are slow to come in, but early indications are encouraging, since the worst of Hurricane Angie missed landfall, staying out to sea. Some roads are closed and shelters are . . ."

"Looks like we're going to survive," Leo says.

"Were you scared?" I ask him.

"Scared," he says thoughtfully. "Not of dying. That hasn't scared me for a long time. But yeah, I was scared. For you."

"Me?"

"Yeah." He turns away from me. "You're my kid. You have a lot of things to do. That's why I worried about you diving this summer. It can be dangerous and you were inexperienced."

"Me." It's a flat statement, all I can think of to say. I'd thought he didn't think I was good enough to dive for Rafe, not that he was concerned for my safety. Does this mean he worries about me when I'm home in Chicago, the way Mom does now, but without the phone calls?

He clears his throat and concentrates on the wheel. "I know what a broken arm feels like."

I'm not tracking too well. How does this follow? But I try to keep up. "You do? When did you break your arm?"

"I didn't break it. I had it broken for me. When I was twelve."

I spread my legs, bracing myself tighter into the corner. Even with the blanket around me, I'm cold enough to shiver. "Sports?" I ask, my attention wandering. I want to lie on the flooded floor and sleep.

"My father."

I wake up. All I know about my grandfather is that he died just after my parents got married. I don't even know what he died of. "Your father?"

"My popular, smooth-talking, drunken, son-of-a-bitch father. He owned a butcher shop. Everybody loved him. Why not? If all you expected of him was that he saved the good lamb chops for you, or got you the biggest Thanksgiving turkey, what's not to love?" He keeps looking forward out the window, where the rain is still gusting, as if he's talking to himself. "I don't know what he was so mad about, but he was—and he saved it for home. I never wondered why my mother left us."

"She left? Why didn't she take you with her?"

His shoulders move. "She left with somebody. Somebody who didn't want kids. She took her chance to get out. I don't blame her."

"You don't?" I feel hot and cold and outraged all at once. I can't stop shivering and my words shiver, too. "She abandoned you. Parents aren't supposed to do that."

"I guess she didn't read the rule book. Maybe she didn't know there was one." He looks over at me. "I didn't either."

"I think I noticed that," I say. I've never imagined having a showdown with my father, rubbing his nose in all the ways he's failed me. He hasn't mattered enough for me to want to do that. Or so I thought. Now that an opportunity seems to be presenting itself, I find myself more than ready for the showdown, but oddly unwilling, not wanting to hurt him, in spite of all the hurt I've absorbed from him. Despite his deep tan and macho swagger, I can imagine him twelve years old with a broken arm. Maybe it's my fevered state, but I don't think that boy needs to be hurt anymore. The difference between him and me could simply be that I had a good mother and he didn't. Without that, I could be headed for the life he has.

"Yeah," he says. "I don't doubt it. That's why I wanted you to live with your mother. She knew what she was doing. I was even afraid to have you with me for two weeks a year. I didn't know what you liked to do or how to find out. I didn't even know how to talk to you." He lifts one shoulder. "I'm glad you're doing okay without me."

I sink down until I'm sitting on the wet floor. I'm soaked through anyway, so it doesn't matter. I pull the wet blanket closer around me. He was afraid to have me with him. Not reluctant. Or resentful. Or angry. "Maybe not right now," I say.

"We're going to be all right," he says, peering through the wet window where dawn is lightening the sullen sky. "We'll be going in now. We've got to get you to a hospital. I think it's safe to anchor in Fortunata again."

I lay my forehead on my knees. My forehead is bruised and it hurts. So do my knees. My eyes close.

I feel anchored already, in a way he never has. I hope that someday he'll get anchored enough to settle. But suddenly I know I'll keep coming to see him, no matter where his anchor falls, or for how long.

I can still feel the impression of his fingers on my ankle.

I sleep.

It's after noon by the time we get back to the dock at Fortunata. The *Angelfish* isn't there, but Leo says it'll probably be back soon from wherever it went to be safe from the storm. Nathan's too good a sailor to have left it in danger.

The sea is still high and the sky dark and swollen with moisture that keeps falling, but the winds are abating. Because of my broken arm, I can't help Leo with the docking, which makes it a terrific struggle for him. Watching him manage it by himself is a revelation to me, an illustration to me of how strong and competent he is when it counts. Maybe a sinkful of dirty dishes isn't such a big deal after all.

He gets me off the *Conch* with surprising gentleness and, with his arm around my shoulders, runs with me through the rain to the truck, still miraculously parked behind his cottage. There are palm fronds and lawn furniture and trash in our yard, blown there from God knows where, and the little beach is completely drowned.

"I half expected to find this sailed into Miami," he says, opening the passenger door and helping me in. "Looks like we took the brunt of the storm out on the water."

My teeth are chattering though it isn't that cold, and my arm hurts all the way into my neck and chest. I pull the soaked blanket closer around me.

Leo gets the truck started and we lurch out of the

muddy yard. "Let's hope the bridges are okay, so we can get you to the hospital."

I guess they are, because when I open my eyes we're in the parking lot.

I'm there for two days getting my arm put back together and my fever under control. Phone lines are down, which means I don't have to explain anything to Mom, who is probably making life miserable for the telephone company in Vienna or Rome or wherever she is. I know that the minute the lines are fixed, hers will be the first call through.

TWENTY-SEVEN

The phone is ringing when Leo brings me home from the hospital.

"You might as well answer it," Leo says, giving me a look. "We both know who it is."

I lift the receiver. "Hi, Mom," I say.

"How did you know it was me?" Before I can answer, she goes on. "Are you all right? I've been frantic. The news is so incomplete over here but, I mean, a hurricane! Right where you are! I warned you. How can Leo live in such a—you are all right, aren't you?"

"I'm fine," I say, using that phrase again. "I had a little accident, but I'm fine, really."

"An accident? What kind of an accident?" Her voice is sharply suspicious. Even long distance, it's amazing the amount of information you can get from the sound of a voice, the part that's most seriously missing from written communication, or from photographs, which makes misinterpretation of them so easy. Somehow she knew I'd had more than a little accident, and it didn't matter what comforting lie I told her, she wasn't going to believe me.

"Well," I say, resigned to the truth, "I broke my arm falling down during the storm. It's all fixed, in a cast. It'll be off before school starts. Don't worry."

Well, she wants all the medical details, most of which I don't know, and she's going to cut her trip short even though it's almost over anyway and come home now for reasons I can't fathom, and she wants to talk to Leo and tell him how careless he's been with me, but I convince her the accident is in no way his fault, that in fact he saved me from making it worse.

When I say that, Leo gives me a somewhat startled look. I smile at him. Then he gives me a *really* startled look.

"And don't come home," I say to Mom. "For what? I'm fine. In fact, why don't you stay longer? I might spend the rest of the summer here."

Honestly, that thought had not entered my mind until I hear it come out my mouth. But it must have been in there—where else did it come from? Apparently my status as community experiment is one I'm as curious about as everybody else. I want to stay until the experiment is over.

Leo gives me another startled look. I've made the assumption I *can* stay, that he isn't anxious to get rid of me. I've made it on the basis of how my own feelings have shifted since the storm, like sand over a wreck. And on account of the things he's told me about his

father and because I want to keep open the door between us for a while longer. I guess I've learned some
risk-taking from Rafe and from Tia.

Suddenly it occurs to me that my assumption is
mistaken.

Then Leo smiles, a rare thing, and gives me a thumbs-
up sign.

Mom sputters and objects and disapproves, but finally I tell her I have to go, that we can talk about it
later, and I hang up.

We sit up late that night and Leo talks to me. I ask
him questions and he answers them, about his parents,
about Mom, about how scared he was of fatherhood—
of knowing what to do. He doesn't look at me when he
talks but at his rough, calloused hands, clasped between
his knees. He chain-smokes the whole time, and I try to
ignore it. He's a lonely, limited man and I may decide
that two weeks a year is still enough, but somehow most
of my anger is gone.

When it's finally time to sleep I sense his relief to
have the questions over. He follows me to my room, and
when I'm in bed, he smooths the sheet over me and
clumsily tucks it in.

"I never did this when you were a little boy," he says.
"I didn't know how."

"Now you do," I say, and I'm asleep in a minute.

The next day we head out in the boats for the first time
since the storm. I can't dive, of course, but there's no
way I'm going to stay ashore.

We're all hoping that the remains of the *Nueva Cádiz*
haven't been moved by the storm out of Rafe's lease sites.

"If they have been," Tia says, "I'll go out at night and move them back, piece by piece."

"You can't do that," I say. "It would destroy the archaeological integrity of the site."

"What, you think Hurricane Angie hasn't done that already?" she asks.

"Hold it," Rafe says. "You're both right. In three hundred and fifty years, how many hurricanes do you think have stirred things around down there? That site's already been disturbed some. But that doesn't mean it's okay to mess it up further. Relax. What's happened to the *Cádiz* has already happened and all we can do is investigate the result. It could be that the storm has uncovered it all for us and it's lying down there bare and beautiful."

"Then we should be out there keeping the *Pelican* away," Tia says fiercely.

"We don't have to worry about the *Pelican* anymore," Rafe says. "She didn't have the good skippering the *Conch* had. The storm blew her into the beach and totaled her. No one killed, but no more boat, and the 'fishermen' seem to have gotten discouraged enough to go back where they came from. What a shame, don't you think?"

Tia smiles, looking like a dusky Renaissance angel. "There is a God," she says.

"That's so, Miss Tia," Nathan says, "but in this case I'd say the hurricane gets the credit."

"Whatever," she says flippantly, and then remembers her resolve. "I mean, I guess you're right. But they could be connected, couldn't they? Anyway, those fishermen are going home with a fortune in gold coins and who knows what else. I'm not feeling too sorry for them."

We get our anchors out and Rafe, Tia, and Nathan go down. Leo stays with me, tending the compressor. I can't do much with one arm, so Leo says I'm just ornamental. He's learning how to kid with me, and I'm learning not to think he's being insulting when he does it.

Suddenly Tia's head breaks the water, her hair curved into curls even soaking wet. She holds something over her head, and when she spits out her regulator, she yells, "I found it!"

I jump up and go to the rail. "Found what?"

"Look." She holds on to the lowest rung of the ladder, stretching up to me. As I take what she hands me, Rafe's head breaks the water, and then Nathan's.

It's a brass plate, the kind attached to traveling chests, lightly touched with green corrosion, dulled but perfectly legible. It reads "*Xavier Ortega Fuentes, Nueva Cádiz, de Cartagena a Madrid.*"

TWENTY-EIGHT

Lisbon has us all over that night. Rafe has reported our find to the state of Florida, which has assigned the Marine Patrol to guard the site until we have more help of our own. He's already been contacted by a couple of TV stations and one magazine. The find is ours now, no doubt about it, so we'll be the ones in the record books. We sit on the porch for a long time, talking about our adventure, celebrating. It's dark when we finally go in to eat, and the dining room is lit just by candles. There seem to be hundreds of them, and the room is full of shadows and wavering light and magic: like underwater.

We hold hands for the prayer, though I can only hold with one and, tonight, we all speak.

Lisbon makes her usual thanks for the company, the success of the hunt for the *Cádiz*, and the improved weather. And Nathan, too, is grateful for the way his life is going, as is Rafe.

Tia says, "I thank You for bringing me an instrument of change," and she squeezes my hand. "And I thank You for making him cute." Everybody laughs except me.

When it's my turn, I'm hesitant, but I say, "Thank You for my broken arm. It changed a lot of things." My head is bowed, but I peek up under my eyebrows and see Leo looking at me.

He's last. He says, in a very low voice, "I'm grateful for Brian's broken arm, too. Amen."

We raise our heads and Lisbon says, "I heard some strange prayers tonight, but I guess I'm not the one who has to decide what they mean. Pass the biscuits."

After dinner we go out on the porch. The flying teeth are in Cuba again and the storm has cooled and cleaned the air. Even the extravagant sunset before dinner seemed fresher and brighter than normal.

Tia and I sit in our place halfway down the steps while the others talk and have their coffee around the wicker table.

"I hear you're going to stay all summer," she says.

"Where did you hear that?"

"Leo to Nathan to Mama to me. True?"

"Yeah."

"Isn't that kind of a change of plans?"

"Yeah."

"Is this a good thing?"

"I think so. Maybe it'll take me the rest of the summer to find out. You trying to get rid of me now that I'm useless?" I flap my arm up and down in its sling.

"No." She lowers her thick lashes. "I'm glad you're staying."

"You are?"

She nods and says softly, "It's good to have a friend around."

"Even a superfluous male kind of friend?"

With her lashes still lowered, she says, "Friends aren't superfluous, of any gender." Then she looks up. "I've been writing about what's happening. We've had an interesting summer so far, wouldn't you say?"

"Yeah, I'd say that. I'm glad you're writing." I run my finger over the back of her hand. She turns her hand and takes mine in it.

"It feels good, doesn't it?" I say, meaning her hand as well as an interest in something outside yourself.

"It does." There's a pause. "I didn't think, at first, we'd get to be friends."

"Me either. You were pretty fierce." I take a tighter grip on her hand, and she smiles, her dimple denting her cheek. "Lucky I'm so hard to scare off," I add.

"Lucky for both of us, I think," she says.

We sit in the dark, holding hands and grinning like fools at each other in the light of the citronella candles.

TWENTY-NINE

Leo and I walk home in the darkness. The moon is thin again and gives little light. But we know the way so well we could do it blindfolded and backwards.

"What do you think we'll find tomorrow?" I ask him. "About the *Cádiz*?"

I sense him shrug beside me. "Impossible to know." After a pause he says, "It's amazing how something buried for a long time can sometimes suddenly be uncovered. It doesn't happen often, but it can happen."

I think he's talking about something other than the *Cádiz*.

"What's amazing to me is how well preserved and shiny some things are, not corroded at all." I *know* I'm talking about something besides the *Cádiz*. "Things you'd never even suspect were there. Total surprises."

"Once you've found them," he says, "it's important

to take good care of them so they last." I sense him turn toward me in the dark, and now I know neither one of us is talking about the *Cádiz*.

"That takes some maintenance. Some attention," I say.

"Sure. But if they're things you value, the effort's worth it. Seems like that'd be obvious, but it isn't always. Just like finding them in the first place. Sometimes seems like more work than it's worth."

"Not once you get the payoff."

"Yeah," he says.

We're at the cottage and I wait while he opens the door. Then he puts his hand on my shoulder and guides me ahead of him across the threshold.

"We're home, son," he says.

I think, Ex Aqua Omnia.